André Caroff's
MADAME ATOMOS

The Sins of
Madame Atomos

*by **André Caroff:***
1. The Terror of Madame Atomos
(translated by Brian Stableford)
2. Miss Atomos
(translated by Michael Shreve)
3. The Return of Madame Atomos
(translated by Michael Shreve)
4. The Mistake of Madame Atomos
(translated by Michael Shreve)
5. The Monsters of Madame Atomos
(translated by Michael Shreve)
6. The Revenge of Madame Atomos
(translated by Michael Shreve)
7. The Resurrection of Madame Atomos
(translated by Michael Shreve)
8. The Mark of Madame Atomos
(translated by Michael Shreve)
9. The Spheres of Madame Atomos
(translated by Michael Shreve)
by Michel & Sylvie Stéphan based on André Caroff:
10. The Wrath of Madame Atomos
(translated by Michael Shreve)

André Caroff's
MADAME ATOMOS

The Sins of Madame Atomos

By
Michel & Sylvie Stéphan

Translated by
Michael Shreve

A Black Coat Press Book

Acknowledgements: Thanks to Françoise Carpouzis & Catherine Losserand.

Madame Atomos Joue sur les Maux Copyright © 2015 by Michel & Sylvie Stéphan & The Estate of André Caroff; English adaptation Copyright © 2017 by Michael Shreve.
Introduction and Timeline, Copyright © 2017 by Jean-Marc Lofficier.
Cover illustration Copyright © 2017 by Jean-Michel Ponzio.

Visit our website at www.blackcoatpress.com

ISBN 978-1-61227-672-4. First Printing. October 2017. Published by Black Coat Press, an imprint of Hollywood Comics.com, LLC, P.O. Box 17270, Encino, CA 91416.
Printed in the United States of America.

Table of Contents

Introduction

The saga of Madame Atomos was a series of 18 novels published between 1964 and 1970 in the *Angoisse* horror imprint of French publisher Fleuve Noir (except for the 18th novel published in 1979 in the *Anticipation* sf imprint).

Our introduction to Volume 1 contains a biography of its author, André Carpouzis, a.k.a. André Caroff (1924-2009), one of Fleuve Noir's most popular authors. More information about Fleuve Noir itself and its popular brands of science fiction and horror can be found in the introductions to Richard Bessière's *The Gardens of the Apocalypse*, Gérard Klein's *The More in Time's Eye* and Kurt Steiner's *Ortog*, also published by Black Coat Press:

Briefly, the saga of Madame Atomos (her real name is Kanoto Yoshimuta) is about a brilliant, but twisted, middle-aged female Japanese scientist who is out for revenge against the United States for the bombings of Hiroshima and Nagasaki—where she was born, and where her family died in the nuclear holocaust.

Madame Atomos seeks to repay the United States by unleashing deadly threats, such as radioactive zombies, giant spiders, a madness-inducing ray, flaming tornadoes, etc., etc. The heroes opposing her are Smith Beffort of the FBI and Yosho Akamatsu of the Japanese Secret Police. In the third volume of the series, Smith was joined by Mie Azusa, the former "Miss Atomos," a younger version of Madame Atomos, initially groomed to continue the fight in the event of her death, but who betrayed her mistress by falling in love with Beffort and, ultimately, marrying him.

There is no love lost between the Befforts and Madame Atomos. She increasingly devotes all her energies to achieve revenge on Smith and Mie for continuously thwarting her schemes. Conversely, the Befforts will do anything to destroy the deadly Japanese *femme fatale* in order to repay her for killing both Dr. Soblen, one of Smith's best friends, and Bob, their baby son.

In Volume 7 of the series, Madame Atomos discovered that her frequent use of teleportation rejuvenated her body, and she now looks like a very attractive young woman. Not only does this help her to evade the FBI, but she uses her charms to seduce Yosho, who is, of course, unaware that the beautiful "Miss Icho Fuji" is, in reality, his deadliest enemy.

There is a real life as well as a fictional gap of almost ten years between the last Atomos novel written by Caroff for the *Angoisse* imprint, *The Slaves of Madame Atomos* (1970), that takes place in April 1969, and *The Spheres of Madame Atomos* (1979), which takes place in 1978.

A few short stories tried to fill that gap: *On an Ill Wind...* (published in Vol. 7) deals with the July 1969 Moon Landing. *A Day in the Life of Madame Atomos* takes place in the swinging London of 1972 (Vol. 9) and *Madame Atomos' Holidays.* (Vol. 9) takes place in January 1976 and shows how the deadly Madame Atomos rebuilt her criminal empire.

But that was it until Michel Stéphan, ably assisted by his wife and writing partner Sylvie, proposed to do a series of novels that would more completely tell the story of Madame Atomos' fearsome exploits during the rest of the 1970s.

Michel was born and lives in Brittany with Sylvie and their two children. He has been a fan of science fiction, fantasy and horror since age 10. In particular, he loves the Universal monster movies (especially the *Frankenstein* series), sci-fi serials and collects Aurora model kits. He is also a regular contributor to our *Tales of the Shadowmen* series, for which he has penned the following stories:

The Stéphans' first novel, *Madame Atomos Sows the Whirlwind*, opens in May 1970, almost a year after the infamous Manson murders in Los Angeles. The second, *Madame Atomos Bets on Death*, follows a few months later, in Nevada. Together, they were translated by Michel Shreve and published in this imprint under the title of *The Wrath of Madame Atomos* in 2014.

This is the third and final novel by the Stéphans featuring the deadly Madame Atomos.

Now read on...

Jean-Marc Lofficier

MICHEL & SYLVIE STEPHAN
d'après ANDRE CAROFF

LA SAGA DE 9
MME. ATOMOS

RIVIERE BLANCHE

ANTICIPATION

BCP

FICTION

Madame Atomos joue sur les maux

THE SINS OF MADAME ATOMOS

Chapter I

Spring 1972

In a small, darkened room a young man was sleeping on a couch. His sleep was obviously troubled and he let out harrowing groans as if he were in the grips of a terrifying nightmare. He kicked violently at the wet, balled up sheets that were half off the bed, which itself looked more like a battlefield than a haven for a fitful sleep.

All of a sudden the sleeper sat up and screamed in agony. Looking disoriented he wiped his sweaty face with a corner of the sheet and glanced around.

These nightmares were getting the annoying habit of recurring. This had never happened to him before. Richard Tardif, an ordinary young man who had lived 25 years with a pretty positive outlook on life, was feeling the return of old demons that he had tried to hide since he was a child.

"What a bunch of crap," he said scrambling out of bed as if it were infested with evil entities. "Nothing makes sense in these dreams!"

Bare-chested before the mirror in his room Richard was totally awake now. Ready to get back to real life, he watched his reflection answer his every whim. He often played at striking poses in front of the mirror and nowadays was spending more time than common mortals admiring himself. But he had a good reason to. Soon he would be a rock star. And the dreams that were troubling his nights were maybe not unrelated to his ambitions.

"I must be in a transition period," he told himself. "I'm becoming an adult and this is obviously what's giving me bad dreams."

There was a moment of hesitation when Richard checked himself out, from head to toe, as if the guy in the mirror was a different person.

"The problem," he went on, "is that I have no desire to grow up. I don't give a crap about adults. Mortgages, wife and kids, no way! I want to keep pissing in the sink and letting the dishes pile up without any female nagging at me."

He started to shave while mumbling the lyrics of a song from one of his favorite bands: "Hang on tight to your dream/When you see the boat go sailing off/Hang on tight to your dream."

This was the message given by almost every rock song: freedom and independence. And Richard had every intention to stick to it.

All of a sudden a particularly hideous nightmare came to mind. The others, the second-rate ones, had completely vanished but this one seemed to be cemented in his memory. In this dream Richard saw his father at his wife's funeral. Chayton Tardif had allowed the body to be buried but he secretly kept his wife's head in a bag, wrapped in towels. It was already starting to rot but the old man protected it like a treasure, determined to make Richard pay for missing his mother's funeral. And Richard heard, in his dream, (or at least he was strongly convinced), his father's footsteps slowly climbing the stairs up to his room. Chayton was holding the gruesome bundle in his hands and his only goal was to swing it around in front of his son's face.

And the dream stopped there, of course. At that moment Richard woke up screaming, which was just the continuation of his subconscious shrieking inside him.

First of all he had to "set the record straight." In truth, his mother was not dead, Richard was sure of this. Or else it must have happened very recently. But if it turned out to be true, he should not feel any guilt over not attending the funeral since nobody had told him about it.

There must have been a deeper meaning to this anxiety. But Richard was no psychiatrist and the dreams were certainly going to go away as suddenly as they had come. There were enough people out there who took a twisted pleasure in making him feel guilty. His subconscious was not going to start on him too!

When Richard had left his native Oklahoma to come to Hawaii, it was not an easy move. First of all because his father, who was very much alive, did not approve of it. Chayton Tardif was a farm worker. He was a man who had never had much luck. But as he liked to say, he was a tireless worker. In the eyes of his only son he was first and foremost a violent alcoholic, and a moron to boot, which seemed to be the norm for a lot of folks living in the cotton belt of Oklahoma.

Many years ago five tribes lived in harmony and shared the Indian Territory. But pooling the lands, a practice borrowed from the Native Americans, was a suspicious system in the eyes of the white colonists. For Oklahoma to become an independent state, the territory could not stay undivided and the lands had to be split up. A small plot of arid soil, therefore, fell into the hands of Chayton Tardif's father who struggle his whole life farming it to feed his family. When his parents died Chayton ended up giving the property away for pennies. Turned into a poor starving Indian he blamed his misfortune on white man's greed and on fate. That was how Richard's father quickly became the slave of a guy who owned more than 1,000 hectares of land and who was kind of enough to give a roof over their heads in exchange for the inhuman work on his farms.

Maybe all the paternal violence and mental debility came from this! Richard, however, had good reasons for thinking that his father was a born loser and that he really had no desire to pull himself out of it.

Richard never knew what exactly happened to his mother. He was too young at the time and he had no clear memory of his childhood. His mother's name was Kirina Chisato. She was Japanese and at the end of the war had started working for the rich land owner. Like his father she was born on the wrong side of the tracks. And like his father she was a farm hand, surviving and suffering with 50 other exploited workers. Richard's father offered her a little more decent housing and she got pregnant right away.

According to what Richard had heard, his parents did not even last one year together. A life scarred by alcohol and violence. By sex, too. All in a more and more sordid environment. The neighbors saved Kirina on the verge of giving birth. When Richard came into the world the circle of friends agreed that he was the product of an umpteenth rape rather than the fruit of love.

The owner, a rather understanding Indian, tried to deal with the problem but this was not the first time he had faced a violent, two-faced worker. He gave him one last chance to straighten up if he did not want to lose his job.

But Kirina had already made up her mind to leave and she abandoned the child who was passed back and forth between the father and the neighbors who tried to take care of him for as long as they could. Farm workers, at least some of them, are people who stick together, who have not been made bitter and mean by poverty.

Strangely, as time passed, Richard's father gradually changed his attitude, becoming more humane, even though he still hit the bottle. Richard could even remember a few happy moments they spent together.

But he was growing up and he could not stay on the farm forever. First there was school and hanging out with other kids. Then there was the army, one year in the Marines, which allowed him to discover other horizons before heading back home and getting the feeling that he was going to start from scratch.

At that point in his life Richard felt like he was running around in circles. He had gone back to his father's house but their relationship had fallen apart again. He had to leave. He did not want to do farm work. In fact, he did not want to do any kind of work. Because working was following in his father's footsteps and he could not stand the idea.

Over the years a good number of workers died and others replaced them, but the family that had sheltered his mother and raised him was still there. When he asked for news about his mother he always got the same answer: Kirina Chisato had completely vanished from the area. Maybe even from the land of the living. She had left a son and this son should not kid himself about her coming back.

Richard had struggled to interpret his dream or rather his nightmare, but he could not figure out what it meant. His father had certainly been violent but he did not kill Kirina. Witnesses had seen her leaving the farm very much alive. As for him, he had no reason to feel guilty about anything.

He threw on a t-shirt and started shuffling around the room looking for something to eat for breakfast.

Through his father Richard had Indian blood and from his mother Japanese blood. This mix gave him a very nice body. He looked a little more Japanese but in a subtle, delicate way, as if he were always looking toward the rising sun. His eyes were slightly slanted and his hair very black, which he cut short. This might seem strange for a young man in the 70s but Richard, like some time traveler, seemed to have stopped in the 50s. He had picked up some strange habits, as much in his taste in music as in his clothes. And he did not care if this made him look like a Martian or a square to the other young people his age. When he left Oklahoma he had sworn that no one would ever tell him what to do.

Coming out of the army he stayed a while dragging his heels around the bigger cities in the state where he was born. He wandered from one to another, left to his own devices. He was not the kind of person to get in fights or break the law and he sometimes had to beg on the street, especially in Tulsa, a city where he lived for a few months. He was going downhill fast, aware that he had to do something with his life or else he would end up in the gutter. So, he made up his mind to go back home. During this period the relationship with his father had got a little better because his old man had damn near calmed down, even though he still took a shine to alcohol. But things could not go on like this forever and Richard felt like he was going nowhere fast.

His dream had been to buy a record store. A cool business for special customers. Only records from the

50s, rockabilly, really obscure stuff that connoisseurs would snatch up! Unfortunately he had no money and not enough motivation to get into any kind of business whatsoever.

And then one day an opportunity came knocking. It was to go to Hawaii where there was a job as a farm worker. But it was not the same work as his father. There were not cotton fields as far as the eye could see. But it was picking. In exchange he would get a free ticket over there, room and board, so nothing to spend at the outset. It was too good a chance to pass up and Richard gave it a go.

When he landed on the island he did not know anything at all about the place. For him, looking in from the outside, Hawaii was all about easy living and nothing else. Although it was true that there were magnificent natural sites on the islands that Richard thought were paradise, he did not come to admire the landscape. He had other things to do.

When his contract was finished, he managed to find a room in Honolulu. But it must be said that it was one of the worst parts of the city. It did not matter to Richard. He was a "cool cat" and he had just found a job, manual labor, hard, physical work, but it had one huge benefit—he did not have to work every day. He just had to show up at the shop, sit on the curb and wait for them to come get him. A big guy came out of the office and pointed to whoever was going to work that day and they took off right away for the work site. It was work on demand and in fact it was perfect for him.

On this particular day he did not go to work. He figured that he had the right since he had worked hard the rest of the week. The important thing was to pay the rent and be able to afford his records, which he was starting to get a pretty impressive collection of, and the clothes that he took meticulous care of. Having grown up among hillbillies, Richard wanted his city threads to be really snappy. The young fashion was more and more scruffy, with those awful bell-bottoms and multi-colored cotton tunics and other things that the 50s would never have allowed. You could listen to rock and play rock but you had to dress with a little class. That was what made all the difference with chicks.

Looking for some breakfast Richard ended up finding a little coffee but his mind was elsewhere. It was the damned dream that put him in this funk!

Good God, his mother's head in a bag! But where did he get all this from? What was his subconscious digging up during the night?

But there was worse. He had heard that dreaming of teeth falling out meant somebody was going to die soon. What a bunch of baloney! He dreamed of losing his teeth and it was for the simple reason that one of them really was about to fall out. An incisor to boot, right in the front! He grabbed it between his thumb and index finger and it wriggled a little. Damn, it was going to come out anytime. He had to go see a dentist. The idea horrified him but it had to happen. Otherwise he would never be able to open his mouth again. Disfigured for life. Okay, he would take care of it today.

Richard stretched and headed for the sink to urinate. It was while he was relieving himself, with his pants around his knees, that the front door swung open.

Susan was bursting into his life but it really was not the best time. She walked in like this pretty often just because he forgot to lock his door. So, she might show up at any time of the day or night. When she saw Richard fumbling with his pants while trying to put on a brave face, a big smile lit up her face.

"You're already up!" she said, heading straight for the pile of records lying on a shelf.

Richard grumbled a response. He hated these intrusions more and more but he was probably just not bold enough to tell her to her face.

He had met Susan through some acquaintances. In truth it was a gang of drug addicts who hung out in the neighborhood and had ended up at his place one night after a lot of drinking to hold a so-called séance to summon ghosts. They had a good time for a while and then Richard had stopped seeing them because he felt too different: he did not do drugs and he hated junkies.

The mistake he had made with Susan had been to call her one Sunday afternoon when he was feeling a little lonely. The girl was really touched because it was the first time a guy had asked her for anything besides powder. Susan was, in fact, the dope connection in the neighborhood. She always knew who and where to get it from. None of this interested Richard who had immediately regretted the phone call. But Susan came to see him and wormed herself into his life.

They had even made love a few times, but neither one of them was really into it.

At first he found it kind of nice to hang out with Susan. She had the same taste in music so they could spend hours listening to rare B-sides recorded by obscure rockabilly bands from the boondocks of deepest, darkest America.

Of course she could not turn up with her gang of spacey friends. Richard had put a stop to that in no uncertain terms and Susan did not seem to mind. They saw each other like two old friends, two partners in crime.

Their friendship gave the young man a little time to breath freely and for her to get away from the junkie lifestyle for a moment.

For, Susan was a junkie, for real. She was a short brunette whose beauty persisted despite her weary eyes. Her body was worn out too from all the abuse. She showed Richard her bruised arms and laughed at his disgusted reaction. The young man did not understand how someone could abuse themselves like this.

He, too, was an outsider. He, too, refused to grow up. But there was nothing in the world that could bring him down so low. It was very important for him to be healthy, so he exercised regularly and figured on keeping his body in good shape.

Susan had remarked that he seemed happy enough with her body when they made love. Richard just nodded. He could find nothing to say to this. Surely just a matter of his sex drive. Susan's hearty laugh filled the room. They were not about to fight over something so trifling. In fact, they never fought.

And although Richard was not always happy to see her just drop by whenever, things always managed to work themselves out because both of them liked to be around each other.

Susan never went anywhere without her cat, a tiny cat called Iggy, who seemed to never get any bigger. The poor thing was pitched left and right at Susan's whim, so it looked glad to find some peace and quiet at Richard's. The cat would squeeze between two piles of records and stay there for hours until Susan decided to leave. Richard had noticed that the little cat was perfectly housebroken. Iggy never wet his room or had any kind of accident. It was not a very annoying animal at all.

"No music!" Richard told the girl who was already putting a 45 on the turntable. "It's too early in the morning. Let me wake up a little more."

"Did you party last night?" she looked surprised.

"No. I just had some nightmares. Which is why I didn't go to work."

Susan was scrutinizing the record covers one by one. "You didn't go to work... and what were these nightmares about?"

Richard was not expecting her to be so intrusive. He thought the question was blunt and inappropriate. He answered in a monotone.

"I dreamt that I threw you out a window, you and your cat, and I watched you slam like shit into the pavement five stories down."

"That's not a nightmare, honey. That's what you want to do in reality."

Still smiling the girl got up and planted a shy little kiss on his mouth. What was really nice with Susan was that he could say whatever he wanted and she never got upset, she always stayed in a good mood.

"Go take your shower," she said. "In the meantime I'll fix you something for breakfast."

Richard said "No thanks" as he headed to the bathroom. He knew Susan too well to know what breakfast meant. While he showered she must have rolled a joint because when he came out 15 minutes later the smell of weed filled his nostrils and made him nauseous.

"Damn! Go and smoke by the window. Your shit makes me want to puke."

"Pete gave it to me," she explained, pretending not to hear him. "He grows it himself. The jerk even made special greenhouses for his plants and he..."

She started laughing and her laugh turned into a cough that sounded like it would never end.

Leaning against the window Richard looked at her. He liked her but they could all go to hell with their weed and all their crap. When Susan was ready to talk again she had forgotten what she wanted to say and silence set in… followed by another coughing fit.

"Okay, you didn't come to see me just to spit out the last of your lungs in my apartment," Richard said. "You got any idea what you want to do today?"

"I could stay here and listen to your records. We could screw a little and if you're nice I could even go out on the landing to smoke."

"I don't hear anything that turns me on. But you and your cat don't bother me at all. We can spend the day together if you've got nothing else to do."

"If only you had a TV. We could turn on channel 5…"

Richard wanted to sound open-minded but he was in a bad mood. The cat was still curled up between the bookshelf and a pile of 45s. At least it was not racking its brain. Richard did not especially like animals. He did not hate them either. He wondered, however, what would happen if he wrapped his hands around Iggy's skinny neck and squeezed with all his might. He had never in his life killed cats. Or it had been a very long time. Anyway, he did not remember. That kind of thing was like a bad dream: he had the ability to forget it after a short time.

Chapter II

Richard was a loner who was constantly traveling in spheres that were inaccessible to common mortals. In the troubled waters of his conscience as they say. When he sat on the sidewalk in the mornings, waiting patiently for the big guy to come out and offer him work, he watched the others who, like him, had come to earn a few bucks.

There were guys who wanted to work for just one day, others who went away cursing the boss when they heard how much they were getting paid. Sometimes there were scuffles, the start of brawls. But none it went very far. Anyway, the whole city was tense and this was not the place that saw the worst of it. Nor the time of day.

For this you would have to wait for nightfall. It was at night that all the lunatics of the megacity came out. This always made Richard laugh, this habit that others had of making the city into window dressing, a symbol of joy and love of life. Surfing, youth, beauty and dough of course. And at night, dope, violence, murders too, sometimes for a measly two dollars, and always dough making the rules on both sides of the fence. What surprised Richard the most was that the idiots seemed to believe in this idyllic vision of Disneyland for the retired. For him who had visited and even bummed around a lot cities on the US, Honolulu was little different from other cities. The same dark side always ended up winning over the sunny side. The nightlife was depressingly similar in every big city; the same sleazy restaurants stinking of fried onions and making you want to eat at any time of the day. Richard liked these places.

He was used to violence, even if he was not violent himself. In truth, he was never beat up. He always stayed on the sidelines—whoever does not want to get whipped can always find a way to avoid the fight. But he had seen plenty of blood spilled plenty of times. Whether in Honolulu, Oklahoma or in the cotton fields where despite the solidarity of farm workers men were a little too willing to get in a fight over nothing.

It was in Honolulu, however, one morning, in front of his work, that Richard had witnessed a scene of rare violence. A black guy, stoned out of his mind, behind the wheel of a brand new Oldsmobile, broke down. The guy jumped out of the car like a jack-in-the-box and started bellowing that his car had dumped him, he lived on the other side of the island and he would rather die than have to walk home. He guy was really freaking out and when a crowd started gathering around to watch the show, finding him amusing, the guy pulled out a huge gun from his coat and put the barrel against his head and pulled the trigger, splattering the front row of spectators. Richard watched the guy drop on the hood of his Oldsmobile and he told himself that he was right to stay safe and sound, up in his private spheres.

Contrary to Oklahoma there were a whole bunch of guys here with really amazing mugs. Something bad buried deep in their soul was oozing up through their face.

There were also gangs hanging around. Richard did not know exactly how many there were but he knew some of the members. Since he had taken up residence in this neighborhood, he had noticed a few things. Firstly, he was not scared and he often left his door open. But this was done inadvertently. Secondly, he had to admit, as surprising as it might seem, these guys respected him.

Him, the yokel from Oklahoma, the loner, the Indian with Japanese blood! At first he had thought it was because he looked like some weird rocker straight out of a film from the '50s. But after a while he had to accept the truth: the respect that others showed him was only because of Anna.

Anna was the other girl he had met in Hawaii. Nothing at all like Susan. First of all because she was a professor, an English professor in fact, which raised her a little above the other. And also because she was not, of course, a drug addict. She was from the right side of the tracks, from the side where people are serious and earn their living honestly. Her family was from the island. Anna was a real Polynesian and her surname meant "bloodstone" in Polynesian. She was not much older than Richard but she acted a lot more mature. This, of course, was not hard to do.

They had run into each other in a bar. Richard tried to hit on her very clumsily and right away she took the lead. She was attracted to him too. She brought him back to her place, an elegant apartment in the hills of West Honolulu and on seeing the furniture Richard originally thought that she lived with her parents.

"A real old fogey home," he commented.

Not a single comic book! Not a single record! Nothing but fuddy-duddy knickknacks and boring books.

They had made love and it took no time for Richard to realize that she was an alpha female, but he did not care. To tell the truth he did not care about sex, with her or anybody else.

As time went by he saw Anna regularly and they became friends. Just like Susan. Except that the young Polynesian hassled him constantly about his way of life and his future. They argued a lot about it since Richard was not ready to change his ways. After a while the kid was forced to face reality: Anna liked him more than he had thought and he felt the same. But each of them was sticking to their guns. It was out of the question for Richard to move in with her with all the differences still separating them. Anna had her world, a professor who hung out with professors, and those people had conversations that were completely beyond Richard. The kid could rattle off the name of all the records from Sun Studios after Sam Philips bought it but he did not know the name of the governor of California. It was Ronald Reagan who had governed the state since 1967 and his film and radio career had made him famous. But Richard was only interested in things he liked and that was what Anna complained about.

Once or twice she had come to pick him up at work because of course she had a car and he did not. It was then that things started to change, that some guys began to talk to him with a glimmer of admiration in their eyes.

"You know Anna!" they often said to him.

Of course he knew Anna! He had even slept with her a few times. True she was beautiful, with her tan and her air of a Polynesian goddess. Well, when she really wanted to look good. Because most of the time Anna seemed to take pains not to show off her charms, as if she could melt into the crowd of mortals more easily. Maybe it was her being a professor that demanded she not be too superficial.

But okay, none of this explained to Richard the sudden respect the boys in the neighborhood were showing him.

And then one day he heard some rumors going round about Anna. Of course they were only rumors. Anna who was asking him to finally act like an adult,

Anna who was worried about his future and who spent their long nights together watching channel 5 to listen to Maella Numi present her masterpieces, this Anna, they said, was part of the Atomos Organization! Right, this was what they said at first. Later the talk was more nuanced. Apparently she was not a potential murderer eager to reduce the United States to ashes. Let's say that from afar, from a certain distance, Anna had something to do with the Organization. Richard did not believe it but one thing was sure: they respected him. And well, if he wanted to have a clear conscience the simplest thing was just to go ahead and ask her.

He remembered the moment he found the opportunity. He had wanted to wait for one of their frequent arguments. Truth to tell, he had even caused a fight so he could talk to her. The young lady had just started in on what seemed to be her favorite topic of conversation: Richard's professional future.

"You're always talking to me like I was a kid," he snapped. "What am I supposed to understand later?"

"You are still a boy, Richard. You're really naïve and pure. That's what I'm complaining about but at the same time that's what I like about you. So don't be so touchy. I just wanted to say that later you'll understand how important it is to plan for your future today."

She touched his arm but he pulled away.

"Don't treat me like a jerk! Maybe I'm a kid but I know about you. Seems you're part of the Atomos Organization."

Anna's expression did not change. She even held back a little smile.

"I'm part of the Atomos Organization! That's it! That's the scoop! And where did you dig up this sensational news?"

"You're part of it or you're in contact with some of the members, I don't really know. In any case, the whole neighborhood knows about it."

"But we don't live in the same neighborhood. And do you believe this story? That's giving me a lot of credit."

"I don't know. People talk. Everyone seems to believe it."

"I never hid my thoughts from you," Anna went on. "You know that I don't hold a special place in my heart for Americans. I could draw up a list of all the abominations they've committed in the name of democracy. But you, except for your records and your culture, sorry I mean sub-culture of morons, you know nothing about anything and I don't think you're in a position to discuss these things with me. You wouldn't understand all the subtleties of what I might say."

Anna's voice had risen abruptly Richard started wondering if he should just leave.

"I'm not chasing after you," she continued. "You can stay and sleep here if you want. And to keep things simple for you I'll just say I support no forms of violence. I'm totally against the fact that they sacrifice human beings for a cause whether it's just or not. But I understand this Japanese woman's actions, even if it sometimes makes me contradict myself. If you showed a little more interest in the politics of your country instead of your culture of shit, we'd have a little more to talk about. Since you moved to Hawaii, it would've been good for you to take a little interest in the history of these islands and the way we natives look at our annexation by the USA and the fact of being just the umpteenth state of America."

He watched the woman whose anger made her even more beautiful.

"All right now, that's enough," Anna finished up. "Go back to bed and we won't talk about it anymore."

Indeed, since that argument, they had never broached the subject again. At least until one day very recently.

A year had gone by since this incident. Anna and Richard continued to see each other but their relationship remained tense. Anna still scolded the young man for his lack of maturity and their breakup became inevitable.

Breakups—there had already been plenty of them. Anna left him a note in the mailbox every time, telling him that it was no longer possible, that they were too different and that she could not imagine building something with an overgrown teenager. Then they got back together and everything started over again.

One night Richard had drunk a lot, which was unusual. He went to Anna's already tipsy and threw himself on the couch in the living room. They ended up talking about Madame Atomos but not that Anna was directly involved in the Organization—even if she was really involved…

The young man had started by counting the crimes committed by the Japanese woman whose deadly attacks had made enough headlines for a guy like Richard, who usually did not give a damn, to hear about them. He had listed Atomos' multiple acts of terrorism, commenting on them with a series of unintelligible mumbling. Seeing that it was going to be a long night, given the drunken state of her friend, Anna went to get a blanket and draped it over the young man who immediately started to fall asleep.

He woke up late into the night. He had had a deep and heavy sleep and he felt fine. The sun had not yet risen when he went to the kitchen to make some coffee. Then he thought long and hard before going to join Anna in the bedroom.

"What's wrong?" she whispered, half-asleep, fumbling for the alarm clock. "I'm sleeping. Go back to sleep yourself and don't make any noise."

"Anna, I've got something important to ask you."

"Can't it wait until tomorrow?"

"No. Anna, can you get me into the Atomos Organization?"

"What? What are you talking about? Stop bothering me about this. Go back to sleep."

"They've got to be looking for manual labor for all kinds of things, for little jobs that need to be done."

Now completely awake she looked at him in the shadows and did not answer. Her cat eyes dilated in the dark.

"I want to prove to you that I'm more than a kid," Richard went on. "I want to show you what I can do. Plus, with your situation you should be able to get me in."

"You're a complete moron, my poor friend. Anna started to smile. "With your situation you should be able to get me in," she mocked. "Listen to yourself! You think I'm the head of personnel or something? That's completely absurd."

"I was thinking you could get me in," he insisted, paying no attention to her remark.

"What's wrong, Richard? Are you in trouble right now?"

The young man did not answer. He climbed silently into bed and slipped under the sheets next to her.

"You used to want a record store," Anna continued. "That's worth pursuing. I could help you. I don't have any money but I know a lot of people. It's doable but you've got to come up with a real project."

She gently caressed his head before realizing that he was asleep. As for her, she had to wake up soon anyway. She had a steady job, a life to lead and nobody was helping her out.

That day Richard did not go to work. Susan the junkie and her cat had stayed at his place but it did not matter. They spent the day doing nothing.

Richard was lost in his thoughts. On the one hand, his nightmares were becoming more and more frequent and weird—not everyone dreams of his mother's head being carried in a sack. On the other hand, there was this record store project that might pan out. Anna was going to give him a hand; she knew people. Only he did not have the stomach for this kind of thing and he was certainly going to screw it up. He mentioned it to Susan who was puffing on her joint. The cat had not twitched an ear for hours.

"You've got no self-confidence," Susan told him. "In my view you should go to therapy. Ten or so sessions and you'll be setting up a whole chain of stores."

Richard sometimes wondered if it was worth the trouble of confiding in this girl who seemed, at times, to have a brain the size of a pea... or who, more likely, did not give a damn about him.

Susan knew all about his relationship with Anna and the rumors about her all over the neighborhood. How could this professor have such a reputation and if it was true why wasn't she already in the pen?

"I'm just wondering what you think of the idea. And none of your lame jokes," he grumbled.

"First of all, if I was in your shoes, I wouldn't let that girl help me. I'd set the whole thing up myself."

"You know perfectly well that's impossible."

"You're in love with her!"

"No, not really. But she symbolizes something for me. A future or… a life raft. I don't really know how to say it…"

"And I'm the one you bitch at for talking crap!" Susan automatically offered him the joint, which he refused as usual.

"Susan, do you believe everything they say about Anna and the Atomos Organization?"

"Listen, apparently Dillinger, in his heyday, when the FBI was looking for him, showed up around Dallas. I wasn't born but my whole family lived there at the time. Well, Dillinger ended up staying there around two weeks, okay, my dad told me all this. Okay, you can believe me or not but from what I hear everyone in Dallas put him up during this period. My dad wasn't the last one to do it. See, when it comes to rubbing elbows with bad guys, we all lie a little. So, your professor, sorry but I really doubt it. In my opinion, the only organization she belongs to is the PTA at her school."

"I see, but that doesn't explain why you don't want her to help me on my project."

"You're starting to piss me off, Richard."

Susan jumped up and grabbed Iggy by the scruff of the neck with surprising brutality. Then she headed for the door. "I was counting on spending a cool afternoon with you and you can't stop talking about that inbred slut!"

Then she disappeared as if by magic behind the door. Richard wondered if the joint had something to do with her fit of anger or if it was really all his fault.

He spent the day drifting through the neighborhood, stopped to drink a beer in a bar where nobody knew him, then bought two newspapers, one that talked about music news and the other about news in general. In any case, he did not have time to read either one. When he got back home at the end of the afternoon he realized that he had forgotten them somewhere but he could not remember where.

In the mailbox he found a letter addressed to him. It was from Anna. Seeing how thick the envelope was, he thought for a second that she was breaking up with him again. But it was nothing like it. The letter was about their recent conversation:

Dear Richard,

Concerning your project to open a shop, I thought it'd be wise for you, if you haven't already done it, to find a good location. It'd also be good to think about the merchandise: what kind of music? What prices? What distributors? Okay, I'll leave it there. Just to say that I'm inviting you over Friday night. I'll introduce you to a friend of mine who might be a good advisor and even an invaluable assistant. It's up to you to rise to the challenge and convince him that you're all in. You can do it... will... motivation... work...

Damn! The letter went on like this for more than a page. He could not believe that an exciting project could become a pain in the ass when it was put like this! Richard was no longer very sure he wanted to open a record store. Some dude was going to explain what he had to do... he should have just shut up about it the other day.

He went to the fridge and popped open a beer, cursing the whole time. Good God, his tooth was still loose and he had not even gone to the dentist.

Anna looked hard at the little man who had just sat down on her sofa. He had a pretty friendly face and yet she could not help getting the willies. Maybe she was making a serious mistake.

Everything had happened so fast since the last time she had seen Richard. He had talked so much nonsense the other night when she was still half-asleep that his name naturally came to mind when the little man had asked her if she knew anyone who fit the profile he was looking for.

It was an unusual request. Such a thing had practically never come up since she first got involved with these people. But the little man had been adamant. There was absolutely no danger for the person to be hired. This guarantee should have reassured Anna but it was far from the case here.

Also, when he shook her hand it was hard for her to hide her worry. The man saw this and tried once again to put her mind to rest.

"Come on, you've really got no reason to worry about your friend. Especially since there's a good chance he won't even fit the bill. Our criteria for this mission are very strict. Don't fret, Miss. We've known each other for a long time now. I think that after all these years some bonds of trust have been established between us…"

Anna tried to smile.

"Very good," he continued. "So, I'll tell you on Friday. I'm looking forward to meeting this young man. I wish you a very good evening, Miss."

The door had not even clicked shut when Anna broke down in tears.

Chapter III

Anna Bernyanyi had good reason not to like Americans. First of all, her family had lived in the Hawaiian Islands for generations and none of them swallowed what everyone called the Yankee supremacy. But she also had personal beliefs that dated back to her college years. At the time the University at Manoa still did not have a department of Hawaiian Languages, which was only opened in 1970, just two years ago. Now they taught the language and culture of the islands, which allowed the students to get back in touch, officially and directly, with the civilization they came from, but when Anna was studying, nothing like this existed. She was dating a guy with a long history in the armed struggle and it all seemed so exciting to her. Violence was justified for political reasons and the exhilaration that came from transgressing the law had slipped into the rather orderly life of the young student. When she thought back on it years later Anna judged harshly this man whom she once loved. He was just another hoodlum, a guy who had seduced her solely with his smooth talk and his deep blue eyes. Eyes that today must be seeing only a sliver of sky through the bars of a cell. At best.

The problem was that this bad company still had consequences in Anna's life years later. Because this guy was mixed up with the Atomos Organization for a time. Not in a high position, for sure! But knee-deep.

At the time Anna's place was occasionally used as a meeting place, but rarely. Long after the guy was arrested, long after their break-up, Anna could not shake free of the strings connecting her to the Atomos Organization. She was marked for life. From time to time some members still used her apartment. Moving did no good: the Atomos Organization found her everywhere.

Well, even if she could not stand this hold over her, she was still on their side. Today Anna condemned all forms of violence, no matter what, which was in contradiction with the acts committed by Madame Atomos. But Anna had no choice: sticking to their ideas while trying to blot out the violence was the only way she could find to look at herself in the mirror, all the while leading an ordinary little life as a college professor.

Anna owned a small house on the island of Lanai, a house that her father (now deceased) had left her. She took a vacation there every time she felt the need to leave the city. The Atomos Organization smelled an opportunity there. In Hawaii there are no real state police. The Honolulu County sheriffs cover the whole, huge island of Oahu where 80% of the state's population live. Despite close cooperation between the various jurisdictions, the other islands handle things the best they can to keep law and order in their territory. For a mafia organization, therefore, it was perfect for a base on one of these islands where the police force was fairly discreet.

In a polite but very firm manner—Anna still had a little scar next to her eye—some agents from the Atomos Organization had come to requisition the house. She was there for only brief periods that were, fortunately, few and far between. She had no choice but to accept.

When she went back to Lanai after the first use by the Organization, she found the house spotless. Nothing looked touched and everything, absolutely everything had been cleaned, disinfected and even sterilized. The unbearable odor of bleach filled her nostrils and it reminded her of death. The young lady was pretty sure that in this family home where she came with her parents as a child, the Organization had brought guys to make them talk or simply to get rid of them.

The house had become a torture chamber and death row. Anna could not bring herself to open the closets for fear of discovering a mutilated corpse. But she never found anything. The Organization did things so well! And Anna, deep down inside, preferred not to know any details.

She wondered why she had been so quick to give Richard's name after he had spoken to her that night. Logically, she had to admit, it was like signing his death warrant.

But no. It cannot all be negative and hopeless in this rotten mess. She herself was still alive, which was proof enough that everything was not so dark. And the little man needed someone and it was not in his interest to put him in any useless danger. Of course there were risks. But there were always risks. Here they were practically zero and there was money to be earned for Richard: $10,000 in his account when he got back from the mission.

Anna thought about all he could with the money, how he could carry out his project, secure his future and how she could help him. Maybe she could even open the shop with him. With so much money they would not have any problems.

Unless there was a scam in the mission like how long it would take? Maybe Richard was going to be away for two or three years and then $10,000 would not be too much to pay! Anyway, there would always be time to turn it down before it was too late.

Anna would have loved to know what the mission was. The little man had told her nothing about it. He just wanted to meet Richard.

The kid was not particularly excited about the meet that Anna set up for him. Meeting this guy was going to make him confront too many realities. Still, he got to his friend's place pretty early so he could talk with her before the guy arrived. But it was a futile precaution: the man was already there.

Anna introduced them rather awkwardly. Richard did not have time to catch his name. Or at least he did not memorize it. Anyway, it was a name that sounded vaguely European.

He was a small, white man, obviously a foreigner, who must have been close to 50 years old, and he did not really look like someone who worked at a bank. Elegantly dressed, he gave off a headstrong air, which impressed Richard quite a bit.

"I'm happy to meet you, Richard. I'll take the liberty of calling you by your first name. But please, sit down."

With a falsely friendly attitude the man took all kinds of liberties, starting with giving orders to everyone. Richard tried to hold his icy glare. Although the guy did not look like a banker, he certainly did not look like Richard's idea of a con artist either.

The conversation began with small talk. The guy asked him about his last name and Richard, who was eager to get to the point, said he knew nothing about it.

Finally the man got around to asking, "Anna tells me that you're thinking of opening a store?"

"A record shop, sir."

Damn! What came over him to start calling the guy "sir"? Richard sat up straight on the couch while Anna, standing with her arms crossed over her chest, looked petrified. If he had been closer to her, he would have seen the beads of sweat on her forehead.

"Only for old 45s. Stuff before the '60s. You know, the era of Sun, Sam Philips… But there wasn't just Sam Philips. We Americans often forget that every state had its own recording studios and any yokel from Arkansas could cut a record at that time."

Good Grief! He suddenly had a desperate hope that the guy did not come from Arkansas. But the little man did not bat an eyelid. He seemed to be listening, to be truly interested in what he was saying. Richard could not get over it.

A smile crossed the man's face, "If I understand you correctly, this project is rather dear to your heart. You might, however, still lack some experience in business. Nonetheless, from what your friend tells me, it's the initial capital that you're in need of."

Both of them were silent. Richard reached for his beer can. The guy had still not touched of drop of his. Richard thought he might be clean like a real professional. Professional of what? He had no idea but he could imagine now that the guy must be an expert in whatever business he was involved.

"That's right. I don't have the money. At least for the merchandise, the piles of rockabilly 45s rotting in attics all over the place. Even here in Hawaii. Well, you're probably going to say…"

The guy smiled again and raised a hand, implying that there was no need to explain something he did not care about. "You know, I'm not as fortunate as you to know about the record business. Besides, I have absolutely no ear for music. On the other hand, I can offer you a sum of money that would allow you a comfortable start on your activity."

"You'll loan me…"

"Not at all, Richard. I'm proposing that you earn it. A job. A perfectly decent job."

At these words Richard understood everything. His eyes wandered over to Anna who was standing stock-still like a marble statue. So, she had not taken his request lightly. She was making him take the plunge. She knew that he was capable. Then Richard's eyes turned back to the little man. He had no fear, no apprehension because the situation seemed too unreal to him.

A quick glance at these three characters in the room would have been enough to see that they were all now on the same wavelength.

The man took out a cigarette case that might have been gold, slid out a cigarette and lit it slowly. Richard was ready to continue the conversation with this guy who understood that he now knew what they were talking about. If the cops busted into the apartment at this moment he was already involved. He was talking to a person, to *people*, seeing that Anna had to be included after all, who were part of the Atomos Organization. Richard would have liked to something stronger than beer because his heart was starting to jump out of his chest.

"We must be clear," the man resumed. "First of all, the task I'd like to trust you with carries no risk. But, as I've already told Anna, there's no such thing as zero risk. That's why you will be well compensated. But during the mission you will run the same risk as sitting on this couch. Because, of course, from this moment on, just talking together, you can be considered a terrorist.

41

Anna told me that I can trust you, that even if you don't fully approve of our actions, like her you agree with the general tenets of our cause."

"How much?" Richard cut in.

"$10,000, which you can collect on your return."

Richard's mouth dropped. If he were trying to hide his emotions, he failed. The man looked away for a minute, pretending not to notice the reaction. This guy was really a professional who knew how to show exceptional tact.

It was Anna who broke the silence. "There's just one detail to go over. In exchange for $10,000 how long will Richard be gone?"

"From the moment he starts his work, which will be the beginning of next week since everything is pretty much ready and he won't have to be trained, well, from the start Richard will be gone for one week, ten days at the most. Including travel time, of course."

"Ten days of safe work for $10,000," the young man said. "It's unbelievable!"

"Don't fool yourself," the man responded. "If you accept, you'll be part of the Organization. That alone could put you in the gas chamber and that's also what justifies the pay. Someone else might demand more, I can assure you. On the other hand, we won't ask anything more of you afterward. It's temporary employment. Let's just say that you'll be part of the Organization once in your life but after that it will be over for good. We'll have no more to do with each other."

The man laughed a little.

"I'll point out, if need be, that this doesn't mean that we're going to snuff you out when the job's done. Look at Anna. She's worked for us for a long time and she's still alive. I'll add something that you're going to like a lot, at least it should reassure you. Don't take it the wrong way. Okay, I feel like you're going to take it the wrong way, but too bad. You're going to get upset with me but then you'll think of the money and everything will be all right. We chose you for this mission, because you're not really... a tough guy. Listen, we've got a bunch of guys working for us on every rung of the ladder. Young ones who are eager, who are ready to die for a cause or for money, guys who have balls, excuse the expression. You're certainly competent to open up a record store or whatever you want to do. You're the perfect example of a nice young man, despite your habits and your weird haircut. And then you've got that Asian look but not too strong. In short, you're absolutely perfect for a very particular mission. And that's why we're trusting you with only one. You don't fit the bill for others. You don't have the guts for it. You understand what I'm saying, Richard?"

"But after? I'll have to live with the fact that I joined the Atomos Organization at one time."

"Never say that name," the guy snapped, almost yelling. "You'll have been part of the Organization and if you ever have regrets you'll have $10,000 to comfort you. As for the rest, given that your mission isn't very risky, I doubt very much that the FBI will come hassling you some day. Now, if you accept, I have something to give you."

"That covers pretty much everything. Except what the mission is. I know nothing about it," Richard remarked.

"You'll be spending a week on the Army base on the island of Okinawa."

Visions raced through Richard's mind. He could not let this guy lose respect for him because of his huge cultural gaps. Okinawa reminded him vaguely of something, a war movie that he had seen on TV. It was also the title of a song by the hillbilly band Dallas.

"Okinawa in Japan, I guess?"

The man held back a look of dismay.

"Okinawa is an island in the Pacific off the coast of Japan. The American Army still has some bases there. But for the moment only one concerns us, for reasons that you have no need to know, obviously. This base is on one of the smallest islands where the Americans have a contingent of more than 500 men. It's not a lot, but compared to the small number of Japanese still living on the island they've got the majority. I'd say that it's practically an American island because the few remaining fishermen all end up, at one time or another, going off to one of the neighboring islands. The GIs, therefore, are isolated. The island is too narrow to build an airstrip, so only helicopters can land there. The vegetation is a little different than the other islands: the American base is surrounded by a thick jungle that isolates the soldiers even more."

"So, I'm going to get on the base as a civilian. I guess you've taken care of everything?"

"The base is a closed system. All its food and other supplies are brought in by the army. The Americans are too scared to catch diseases by eating Japanese fish. They do, however, have some dealing with a few local businesses for laundry and other stuff that the army can't take care of. But it was hard to get you a cover with them. We've got agents who looked for the best possible way for a man to stay on the base for a few days without attracting attention. Because, you see, Richard, we need someone to stay there long enough to get a good look at all the rooms and basements, even just a quick look, and

44

draw up a map, maybe not complete but precise enough for us to prepare a possible action."

"You're planning to blow up the American base on Okinawa?"

"That's not your problem! Your mission is just to bring us back a map, as detailed as possible. What we do with it is none of your business."

"And you've got a completely safe gimmick for me to play spy?"

"You could say that. The base is built in the middle of a virgin forest. The Americans had a lot of work clearing the land and making the place livable. But there's an insect, or rather a family of insects, infesting the jungle. The bug is tiny but it attacks some under-ground pipes of the base. If nothing is done about it, the little beast might get in everywhere. They've known about the problem on the island and they developed a product that deals with the problem pretty well. The ar-my, therefore, decided to strike a deal with a local com-pany to disinfect the base. It'll take a few days because all the rooms have to be treated and gone over more than once. So the army's letting a worker come live on the base during the operation. You see, nothing could be simpler."

Indeed, looking at it from this angle, Richard had to admit that there did not seem to be a great risk. Anna, too, seemed to relax a little. She had joined the two men and was squatting at the low table, picking at some of the snacks there like she was at a faculty meeting.

"But... well, I don't know anything about disinfect-ing," Richard said. "They'll start asking me questions if I'm on the base for a few days."

"You'll leave in a week, maybe more, depending on several factors. Right now you'll start intensive training and we'll give you a brief medical exam." The man turned to Anna. "We're going to need your house on that charming island again, Anna. We're bringing Richard there to explain everything in detail."

The young lady could not help shivering. The house spooked her and the thought of Richard staying there was hard for her to accept.

"Then we'll bring you back home. Not for long. I think it'll be done quickly. You'll be contacted and leave for Okinawa in no time. But I can assure you that when the time comes, you'll know everything there is to know about extermination."

Richard listened. For the moment he had no questions. He glanced at Anna. Her face looked undisturbed but the way she was unconsciously rubbing her hands and cracking her knuckles showed how stressed she was.

For his part, was it too late for him to turn back? The simple fact of knowing this guy who had come to offer him a mission for the Atomos Organization was proof enough that he could not pull out now. The die was cast. Besides, there was the money to guarantee a better future.

He looked again at Anna and stared hard into her eyes. The last time he had this kind of reaction was on the plane coming into Hawaii. There had been some bad turbulence that lasted longer than usual and the other passengers were keeping calm but he stared at the stewardess trying to detect the slightest hint of worry in her eyes. This was exactly what he was doing right now.

"Can we count on you, Richard? Are you interested in our offer?"

"If I think of the money and only the money, I'm interested. I have to admit that I've never had that much in all my life."

"Plus a week-long trip when you'll discover the charms of Okinawa. No, I won't lie to you, my boy. Spending a few days on an American base won't be a holiday. Moreover, there are a bunch of mosquitoes and strange bugs there. But that's the price to pay. Am I right?"

"There's one last thing that worries me before starting to work for you…"

"But you've already starting working for us!" the little man declared.

Richard immediately understood all the menace this statement contained. "Yes, I get that. I mean after… or right now… or soon when I leave… or let's say… tomorrow morning on waking up, okay, let's suppose that I'm pulled out of bed by two FBI agents…?"

"Yes, I see what you're trying to say. Don't worry about it! For the moment there's no way the FBI knows about your existence or that we've met."

"But Anna? She might get in trouble. And later, when I've finished the mission, what'll happen?"

"Once again, I see exactly what you mean," the guy from the Organization nodded. "And it's good to think about this. I was just getting to this delicate subject."

The guy put his cigarette in the ashtray and from his coat pocket he pulled out a small, rectangular box. It looked just like his cigarette case. It, too, seemed to be made of solid gold. The man opened it and took out a metal cube that he offered to Richard, putting it in the palm of his hand. The young man held it between his thumb and index finger, trying to guess what it could be used for.

"Take a good look," the little man said. "There's a tiny push button on one side of the cube. If you press it, a little cyanide capsule will come out. You should keep it on you at all times. Every member of the Organization has one. It's the answer to your question. If the FBI comes knocking at your door one day, which I pray will never happen, of course, it's obvious that you can't give them any information. Welcome to the Organization, Richard!"

The young man placed the cube gently on the table as if he were refusing the poisoned gift. He was fully aware, however, that it was too late to say no and he understood that he had just jumped headlong into the wonderful world of adults.

Chapter IV

The next day, Richard went to the Manoa airport where a private helicopter was waiting to take him to Lanai. His initiation was about to begin. He had often taken small planes to travel inside the US and he figured that a helicopter ride would be pretty much the same. But when the copter took off, he instantly felt sick, which did not leave him the entire the trip.

The island of Lanai is located between Maui and Molokai. It was bought in 1922 by the king of canned pineapples. This man, who never did things halfway, had transformed most of the island into a pineapple plantation. Richard was in a position to know because Anna had often suggested to him to go and work there. Anna always had good ideas but he had no desire to become a farm worker.

Everything on the island was controlled by pineapples. The fields were all squared off and the little huts for the Filipino workers presented a startling contrast to the luxurious hotels for tourists. The house that Anna's parents owned was built on the other side of the island, in a quiet place called the Garden of the Gods. The quasi-lunar landscape was full of weird rocks that changed color depending on the light.

When Richard got there he was led directly to the house. It was remote, far from the other houses. While the helicopter was flying over this part of the island Richard saw that he was heading toward an uninhabited zone where they landed on a crude airstrip specially built in a clearing behind the house.

He waited in a holiday bungalow and was surprised to find it so big, without being too plush. The guy he had met at Anna's was waiting with him. It seemed he never dropped his high-class attitude: even here, despite the sweltering heat, he wore his elegant city suit.

"It's not yet noon" the man observed, shaking Richard's hand warmly. "I think today's going to be particularly hot. In fact, I still haven't introduced myself. My name is Jack Corso and I'm going to be your tour guide, or rather your coach, during your stay here. Later, others will take over, but let's not get ahead of ourselves."

The walls of the house were very thick and inside it was cool and refreshing. Jack Corso brought Richard into what seemed to be the living room, a big, strangely empty room where he had a hard time imagining Anna rest and relax during her vacations. He was suddenly aware of the fact that she had never spoken of this family home, maybe because the Atomos Organization had made it a kind of headquarters. The room stank of disinfectant. Richard figured that it would be pretty nasty to have to live here for any extended period of time.

Jack Corso gave him a tour of the house, then took him to his room. The first thing the young man did was open the window to air it out.

"Okay. I have to explain something to you, Richard. If you need anything at all, you have to ask me. You can, of course, walk around the house and in the yard as much as like. There's plenty to eat in the fridge so I'll let you take care of that because as you'll see there's nobody to cook for you."

He glanced briefly at his watch.

"Anyway, you're going to be busy. An hour from now Ronald'll come to take over. He's the one who's teaching you everything you need to know to carry out your mission. You'll have to put up with him for two afternoons, only one if you prove to be a particularly apt student. The third day's for your medical exam with vaccinations and a general check-up, etc. Do you take drugs, Richard? Do you drink?"

"No, no, not at all."

"Now something else. I mentioned it yesterday. Look out the window. Good, now, you see a bunch of cop cars showing up. What do you do?"

Jack Corso did not give him time to answer. Without hesitation or gentleness he started searching Richard's clothes.

"Where's the capsule, Richard? You brought it with you, I hope?"

"Damn, man, stop feeling me up! Give me some time to get it!"

He took out the metal cube from one of his pockets and waved it triumphantly in front of Corso's face.

"That's good," the man said. "You didn't forget and you have it on you. Ronald will teach you the best way to hide the capsule on you. Because from now on, Richard, you can't ever leave it behind. It can come in handy for you so you'll have to learn to live with it, so to speak. With what's inside it, you can kill yourself. And under certain circumstances death is freedom, believe me. Anyway, this cube is our guarantee."

"Does Anna have one, too?"

"Of course, Richard. And you can be sure that she wouldn't hesitate to use it if necessary."

Ronald was a giant, six and a half feet tall, and at first sight looked like a mindless brute. But in truth he was a lot more intelligent than he let himself appear. He was an excellent instructor and a shrewd psychologist.

Ronald set the young man straight on a number of scores.

First of all, he taught him a few basics of geography. Richard, *a priori*, did not understand why it was important but he was quickly able to point to Okinawa on any kind of map.

Then Ronald got him using the spray and taught the young man some technical vocabulary that would pass him off as a professional in insect annihilation.

"It's a little like being in the first space capsule," he explained. "You won't have a lot to do. Just go where it takes you. What you're doing is really important to us but it carries absolutely no risk. There's one of our men who lives on the island and he'll get you on the base. They'll think you're an exterminator so when you're alone with the Marines you just have to discreetly get the lay of the land and you can spend the evenings playing cards and laughing at their stupid jokes. That, I admit, will probably be the hardest part of the mission."

He had a jolly laugh, which made Richard laugh as well. All things considered, Ronald was a much nicer than Corso.

"You'll see, it'll be easy. You won't even be searched when you enter that goddamn camp. The Americans are undoubtedly completely paranoid, but they never search civilian workers coming to work on the base. Okay, for you it's true that it's a little different. You'll be staying there a few days and carrying this cyanide capsule on you. We talked about it for a long time and I don't agree that you should have the stuff. But there are orders so I have to give in. At the start they thought of putting it in a hollow tooth or someplace else in your mouth but you would've flipped out for sure. Imagine eating their nasty food in the mess and just dropping dead. The Yanks would be scared that we'd blame their food. Ha, ha, ha!"

He had a good laugh at this for a full two minutes until he started coughing up phlegm.

"Okay, jokes aside, they found a way. It won't make any difference but it's more sensible. It'll be like James Bond. I'm sure you'll dig it. The capsule's going to be put in the heel of your shoe. Like that, out of sight, out of mind."

The giant thought for a minute as if he was about to leave without saying another word. But he continued in a serious tone, "I think we've just about covered it, little guy. How old are you?"

"25."

"Yeah. Don't get too worked up. I see you're nervous and I understand why. But there's practically no risk of screwing it up."

Ronald went to the fridge and grabbed two beers. He put one down in front of Richard. "It's a sweet life we've got here in this pad, eh? Look, it's not always like this but here it's pretty cool. Keep in mind that I'm trying to put myself in your shoes, kid. It's a trial by fire, for sure, and you must be shitting bricks right now. Adrenaline pumping... You'll see, when that adrenaline lets loose, when you're on the base, I'm sure you'll pull it off like a champ."

The young man appreciated the fresh beer cooling his dry throat. Even in the shade and protected by the thick walls, the temperature was still rising.

"So, we done here?" Richard asked. "You've taught me everything I need to know?"

"Yeah, I think so. Tomorrow you'll get your medical exam and deal with some administrative formalities. That's not my department. Sorry, there's no pretty nurse to take care of you but only Dr. Sinclair. A lot less sexy, I admit, but he knows his work and that counts for something."

"And then you'll take me back home, if I got it right, to wait for the big trip?"

"Right, we'll take you back home. But first you have to visit a very important person who wants to meet you before you leave."

Ronald looked amused by the effect this information had. Richard's face suddenly changed color.

"You didn't think you'd get off that easy, did you, kid? There's someone who wants to meet you before you leave us. It's a woman."

The young man did not say a word.

"And if I tell you that this woman is Japanese, it should keep you from asking any stupid questions."

Ronald jumped up from his seat. "Well anyway," he said. "Starting from now you're off duty and me, I'm tired. I advise you not to go to bed too late. You've got a long day ahead of you tomorrow.

Corso was having breakfast on the little patio that faced due west. From here the view was relatively free to see the turquoise blue sea. Richard sat in the armchair across from him.

"This might seem surprising," the little man swept his hand over the immensity of the Pacific, "but there are not enough waves here to surf."

The table was piled with food that Richard did not find particularly appetizing for breakfast. He tried to clear a little space in front of him.

"I need to eat in the morning," Corso went on. "It's often my only meal of the day. You never know what'll happen next."

His plate was full of all kinds of cheese and he was holding a huge sausage that he had dipped lavishly in a jar of mustard.

"There should be something to your taste on the table. You just have to search a little."

Richard poured himself a cup of coffee and sank comfortably back in his chair to admire the panorama.

"As I was saying, the sea is rather calm here. It's partly because of the current that breaks the waves about a mile off the coast. They don't really have time to curl. As a result, the area's better for fishing. Did you know that pineapples abound here? Have you heard of the Dole Company, financed by the king of canned pineapples?"

Richard shook his head and put a finger in his mouth. No doubt about it, his tooth was looser and looser and he still had not gone to the dentist.

"Is there a dentist on the island? My tooth is going to drop out anytime and I'd like to take care of it before leaving."

"You've already got enough things to do today," Corso replied. "You can get your pearly whites straightened out when you get back."

Richard kept wriggling his tooth. The pain was starting to come in spurts and he could not eat without doing acrobats with his mouth.

"You can ask Ronald to plug you in the jaw—that should fix the problem for good," Corso snickered.

Richard did not find the joke very funny. The little man had more style when they had met at Anna's.

"No, it won't be possible," Corso's voice was more serious. "Unless Dr. Sinclair can deal with it. But he's not a dentist."

"I thought you might want to put in a bogus tooth for the cyanide capsule."

"That's a bogus idea and we'd have to call in a dentist for that. No, forget it, kid, we don't do that here."

Richard did not press him. He was concentrating on every mouthful that he chewed very carefully so as not to bother his sensitive tooth. With a little practice he managed to eat without too much pain.

He made up his mind not to talk to the little man about his upcoming meeting with Madame Atomos. Ronald might have been pulling his leg. If not, she would already be on the island or even in the house. But Richard was wary of asking Corso about it.

"How long do I have before my appointment with the doctor?"

"You'll see him this afternoon. But don't go wandering off. We might need you before then. Stay in shouting distance."

At loose ends, Richard shuffled around the garden until he stopped short in the middle of the path. He suddenly noticed a figure behind a window on the second floor. A woman's figure topped with long brown hair. There was too much glare for him to make it out clearly. Too much distance too. The young man started forward. The shadow did not try to hide or move from the window. It was Richard, on the contrary, who was scared. Scared of knowing the identity of this shadow.

The woman was still not moving. And yet she must have seen him and known that he could see her.

He kept walking slowly toward the house, trying to see if the face bore any Asian features. He was only a few feet from the house now, so that he had to look up and strain his neck. Then the figure disappeared. But he had had time to catch a glimpse of the eyes and a peek at the face. And there was no doubt about the identity of the woman.

A wave of heat surged through his body.

He decided to go back to his room and stay there until they came looking for him. The woman might not have come just for him but she was here and their meeting was inevitable. He lay down on the bed and heard nothing but the beating of his heart, which sounded too damn fast.

The afternoon schedule was indeed busy. It started with a serious of cardiac tests: stress test and electrocardiogram. Richard had already had this kind of routine exam when he was in the army.

Dr. Sinclair was a somber, broody man. The only words he mumbled to himself were inaudible. He seemed to be a conscientious doctor and Richard got four shots without batting an eye. No doubt the vaccines that he was in no position to judge their efficacy.

"Everything is in order," the doctor muttered.

Richard knew that he was talking to him this time and he risked a question. "I'm fit for service, I guess?"

"You're in perfect health," the doctor answered without dropping the solemnity that he had shown from the start. "We're done here. Do you want the results?"

"That's not necessary," Richard started getting dressed. "I trust you. I think my stay on Lanai is coming to an end.

Sinclair brought the young man into a room that Richard thought was a little big for a doctor's office. Then he remembered that he was in a vacation home. It was Anna's parents' house and not a doctor's office. The doctor left him alone.

Papers were scattered over the desk. Richard cast a quick glance at them and noticed that they were medical notes without any particular interest to him. He stopped looking at them, afraid that he had done something wrong and he did not want to be caught red-handed in a screw-up.

He was getting impatient and started pacing the room. This reminded him of the endless waits he had had in all kinds of places like this.

When the door finally opened, he let out a sigh of relief. None too soon! Then he froze as if he had just been jolted with 10,000 volts. She was there, ten feet away from him!

Well, this is it! Richard thought when his brain snapped back to normal. *It had to happen since I'm part of the Atomos Organization. I had to meet her someday.*

The Japanese woman closed the door without making a sound. She was not particularly tall but she radiated intense charisma. It must be said that for Richard, who had heard of the damage done by this woman on American soil, Madame Atomos was a kind of an imaginary character. Almost a myth. So, seeing her in flesh and blood standing in front of him caused his brain to misfire. He stood there slack-jawed, staring vacantly at her, without realizing that his whole body had gone numb.

However, she was dressed like a mere mortal. She wore a khaki coat and pale green pants that came straight out of army surplus. Nevertheless, the outfit did not make Madame Atomos look like a warrior or soldier. You would have thought she was out mowing the lawn and wanted to take a break.

The Japanese woman cracked a smile and walked toward him, holding out her hand.

My God, she was so beautiful! Her hair, her eyes… How old was she? 40, maybe more… who cares! This woman glowed and had nothing evil about her.

Her eyes are intense but her face isn't hard, Richard mused, trying to shake some feeling back into his body so he could grab her offered hand.

"I was eager to meet you before you left," she said. "From what they told me you are exactly what we're looking for. Do you feel ready for duty now?"

"Your men explained everything to me," Richard babbled. "I just had my medical exam. It looks great."

"Well, it looks great to me, too. You seem like a charming young man. A handsome, charming young man."

Damn, wasn't there any water in this room? Something he could drink? His throat was so dry that he could not talk.

The Japanese woman walked around him slowly while he stood stock-still, straight as a fence post. He prayed with all his heart that the inspection would end quickly.

"Well, well, Richard, I'm delighted to see you. Do you have any questions for me before we part?"

Although his body felt heavier than lead, Richard's brain was working overtime. He hurried to speak while his vocal chords were still working.

"It's about my tooth," he said. "I talked with your men and they told me that it's out of the question. I have a toothache. It's going to fall out. I'd like you to do something about it before I leave. If you can, of course…"

The woman came up close and asked him to open his mouth. He was already sorry that he had made such a stupid request. She wriggled his tooth with her index finger, whose perfectly manicured fingernail he could observe.

"That hurts?" she asked.

He nodded. She took a small telephone out of her pocket. A tiny, cordless device, quite ingenious, with which she could talk to Corso, Ronald or Dr. Sinclair in a range of around a mile.

"Corso," she ordered, "you're going to take Richard to the dentist. There must be one around here. I want him to leave in the best possible condition. Do it fast so nothing gets in the way of his mission. I'm counting on you. Thanks."

It had been a short call. The young man could not believe it. If he survived this adventure, he could say, one day, that Madame Atomos in person had made a dentist appointment for him.

Called in on the emergency, the dental surgeon had done what he could. The result, although temporary, was satisfactory. Richard figured that his tooth would not bother him anymore, at least until the mission was over. After that, of course, it might be different. But he had time to think about it.

The helicopter took off early the next morning.

Corso and Ronald went back into the house. Only Dr. Sinclair stayed outside to watch. The Japanese woman was at his side, looking up at the helicopter flying away until it disappeared completely from their sight.

"There you go," the doctor said, "carried out as smooth as silk."

"Let's hope so," she responded. "Even though nothing's really started yet... Let's get back in. I got up at dawn and I didn't have time to eat breakfast."

"I understand you, Kirina. It's not every day that you come face to face with your own son."

Chapter V

Richard was back from Honolulu and once again in his studio apartment. He only had to wait for the instructions that would come the next day at the soonest or at the latest before the end of the week. In the meantime he had to be on war footing. Ready to go.

A little like in 1944 when the Americans had landed in Normandy. Richard had seen a report about it on TV and they explained that the guys had a lot of problems setting a date for the landing. Problems with the weather, with coordinating the troops... But here, really, he was all alone. Still, it made him think of D-day.

On the other hand, for this first day Richard was free and clear. If he wanted, he could go see Anna and even spend the night with her. But for the moment this did not turn him on. Maybe later.

He studied the shoes they had given him. Hiking boots, flexible and sturdy. The outside of them had a bunch of stuff: buckles, things to fasten tight the leather laces, straps. And inside a little pocket was hidden, not in the heel like Ronald had said but in the front under the thick sole, right at the toe. The little pocket had a tiny zipper, completely invisible. Richard inspected the shoe, opened and closed the zipper and took out the small cube that he did not feel at all while walking. He was stunned to see himself in possession of such an object, astonished also at the clever camouflage, and then a little panicked by the thought of having a capsule of lethal poison on him. He opened the cube and plucked out the capsule.

"I swallow this and one second later I'm a goner. Painlessly."

That was what he kept repeating, "Painlessly. This capsule will kill me painlessly."

He felt better putting the capsule back. Accidents happen so fast!

They had also given him a small bag with the various papers he had to hand over to the guys waiting for him in Okinawa.

His cover had one big advantage: he would not have to lie much. Once inside the base he would not have to pass himself off as a native. Besides, Richard did not speak a word of Japanese. His role was as an American dispatched to the island for an extermination job. A guy trying to earn a few extra bucks so he could turn around and go home. Therefore, he would not have to worry about getting caught in telling God knows what lies that he would not believe and could only confuse him. He was coming from Hawaii and he was going straight back to Hawaii. It was much more simple like this.

He stood at the window and stayed there for a long time, watching the spectacle of the street. He was aware of how unbelievable his situation was. All the anonymous passers-by he saw rushing around like busy ants had a normal life, but he was part of the Atomos Organization. Right now in Honolulu there was only one guy working for the Organization and he was about to leave for a mission on the American base in Okinawa. This guy was him!

Richard had heard of Smith Beffort, the cop, the FBI guy who was a real-life hero in the eyes of the average American. He spent his life fighting Madame Atomos. Richard knew that he represented a danger to him. *Damn*, he thought, *I'm a threat to all of America!*

When night fell, after a day that seemed very long, Richard had finally decided to pay a visit to Anna. Plopped on the couch they watch television together. The young lady had turned the sound off.

Their relationship had changed. She was a stranger, distant, but Richard understood that Anna was probably sorry that she had spoken to the Organization about him. Still, one thing was sure: they were both stressed and this stress would last until he got back from Okinawa.

A pale brunette, skin like a corpse and the face of a ghoul, appeared on the screen. Richard had often watched this show when he was at Anna's and he recognized it right away.

"That's Maila Nurmi," he said. "They're always showing the same old junk on reruns. Can you turn up the sound, Anna?"

"What'd you call her? I think she's Vampira."

"Vampira is her TV name but her real name is Maila Nurmi and she's been retired a long time. You know my friend Susan, right, the one who's always toting around her awful cat?"

"Sure. At least I know her by sight."

"Well, she got me hooked on this chick. Turns out she's retired here in Honolulu. She knows a bunch of people and has a reputation for being as whacked out as her character. Susan knows where she lives and has offered to introduce me."

"What'd you think of the house on Lanai?" Anna abruptly changed the subject.

"It's a beautiful vacation home and the yard is really huge…"

"That's true. And everything went all right? Did you meet a lot of people?"

"There was that guy I met here with you the other day, Corso. And then a guy named Ronald. And a doctor."

Richard held back from telling her about Madame Atomos. He figured his meeting with her was too absurd, too unreal. A long silence fell over them again. Neither of them wanted to express their thoughts. They settled on small talk.

"You leave in a week?" Anna ended up breaking the silence.

"That's right. A week, 15 days max. It's better that I don't tell you too much. I'm kind of on cloud nine and I wonder if there's a hole in the cloud."

"Aren't you scared?"

"Don't worry. And especially don't blame yourself. After all, it's me who kind of forced your hand that night. Just think how much dough I'm going to rake in and I'll be able to set up on my own."

Anna had a hard time imagining that things were as simple as Richard believed. Entering the Organization was one thing, leaving was something else. She was in a position to know. It had been years since she had been caught in the net and she felt like a prisoner for life.

Of course her bank account, far from being fat, was more comfortable than her university colleagues. And she had to admit that her everyday life was relatively undisturbed. This said, she had to kiss her house on Lanai goodbye, even if no one had ever forbidden her to go there.

The best proof that she was sailing more troubled waters than common mortals was the cyanide capsule that she always carried with her. Anna knew that Richard also had one. Still, with the money he was going to get they could both imagine a future together, which was not possible in Richard's current situation. Anna was not sure of his intentions but this was what she wanted. She loved Richard and was hoping to lead a normal life with him, maybe even have children. *Definitely* children.

And then, looking at the big picture, the mission seemed pretty easy. What Richard had to do was not very complicated. There was no risk of him getting in over his head and aborting the mission. But the danger, even if minimal, was still there. And the young lady felt scared stiff at the thought of it.

Anna put the empty cans on a wooden tray. They had drunk a lot of beer but it did not manage to lift their spirits. A dark mood loomed over the evening.

While she was taking the tray back to the kitchen Richard suddenly announced, "I also met Madame Yoshimuta in your house on Lanai."

There was a moment of silence. Anna came back, still carrying the tray, which she put on the table.

"You mean Madame Atomos."

"Yes, Madame Atomos, that's right. I had the honor of meeting her on the island. We talked. She gave me the rundown on my mission." Richard forced himself to look completely neutral. "She even made an appointment with the dentist for me. Here, look at my tooth. It's not moving anymore."

"Are you sure you're not mistaken?"

"I don't see how I could be. I'm part of the Organization now. It's normal to talk with your boss."

"I can't believe it!" the young lady exclaimed.

For Anna as well, Madame Atomos was a mythic figure. Too legendary, too untouchable to go visit the house of an underling, even for a short time. Richard, however, was right. For an employee to cross paths with his boss was not unusual.

"What was she like?"

"Pretty fascinating, I have to say... Pretty fascinating." After another moment of silence he said, "Well, I have to go now. They're probably going to contact me tomorrow so I have to be at home. While I'm gone maybe you could go by once or twice to pick up my mail and make sure everything's okay?"

"No problem. I still have a copy of your key."

Richard gave her a kiss on the lips and another on her forehead.

"We won't see each other for a couple of weeks. When I get back we'll talk about my future projects. If you're still willing to help me, that is."

"Yes, of course, Richard. We'll talk about all that again. Be careful and try not to pull an Abbot and Costello in Okinawa."

They laughed together. Not that the joke was very funny but the mood was so dark that they needed to leave each other on a good note.

"I'll be more like the three Stooges. It's better."

Anna closed the door behind him. Automatically she started cleaning up the living room, a nervous smile frozen on her face.

He was still half asleep when he became aware that someone was in his room. He heard padded footsteps, then the door quietly opening and closing. Then nothing.

Richard fell back asleep and had a disturbing dream in which he was an explorer in the jungle. In Okinawa certainly. A tiger jumped on his chest, throwing him to the ground, ready to rip off his head.

He was startled awake. In fact, there was a feline on his chest, battering his face with its coarse tongue. It was Iggy showing his affection by licking him.

"Shit!" Richard jumped out of bed. "She better not have done it. Not today."

Susan had left a note on the table. Richard was used to her way of doing things. Usually it was not a problem. But today was really not the day.

"Shit! Shit!" he stormed around the room. "At least she could have woken me up."

Sometimes Susan paid a visit to her parents who lived on the other side of the island. Generally she stayed for three days and left her cat with Richard. The animal was clean and practically took care of itself. So, on normal days it was fine. But today was not a normal day.

I'll have to kick it out, Richard thought. *She left me no choice.*

Then he changed his mind.

Okay, if she's back in three days, it won't be a tragedy. I just have to set up a litter box so he doesn't piss all over my stuff.

When he had finished, he sat in a corner of the room and started waiting. He did not have a telephone and it had been arranged that some members of the Organization would come get him. At any time of the day or night. They could pop by any minute now. But Richard was ready.

Iggy had found a bright red lighter in a corner of the room and was playing with it, jumping around excitedly. The young man watched the cat's movements. With no thought to the laws of gravity Iggy was lost in his precious games. Sometimes he leaped on a shelf with mind-boggling speed but without knocking anything over. At the moment the little black cat missed a jump and plopped to the ground. It was the first time that Richard had seen it fall flat on its face.

"Poor thing, you're getting clumsy."

The cat went straight back to its impromptu game. Then it froze in the middle of the room. Very slowly Richard reached out, grabbed the two ends of the small rug and folded it over the cat. Iggy was captured for a few moments, then it swiftly freed itself, more excited than ever. Richard started the operation over again and every time the cat went back into the middle of the rug as if taunting his new playmate.

Richard was also starting to have fun. From the other side of the room he threw whatever he could grab toward the cat. First a pillow, then a book, then an empty 45 sleeve. Every time the animal dodged the missile nimbly. But it still ended up getting a magazine full in the face, which made it jump but did not calm it down one bit.

The young man stood up and started chasing the cat. Without knowing whether this was still a game or if it was moving onto some other level. Iggy went into attack mode, then jumped back into the middle of the rug.

"So, buddy, you haven't had enough? You've haven't been caught in the rug enough? You still want me to roll you up?"

This time he held the two edges very tightly together. Iggy was thrashing about inside but Richard was protected from its claws by the thick wool. When he opened it up the little cat was still on its feet but it looked completely groggy. Maybe from a lack of oxygen. It was slowly catching its breath.

Richard took the opportunity to close up the rug again, holding the edges firmly against the floor. He had the vague feeling that the game was becoming a little twisted but he could not resist the desire to put the animal in a more and more dangerous situation.

When he finally decided to let the cat go, it was obvious that it needed a lot more time to recover than before. Richard's excitement was becoming uncontrollable. In fact, he did not really know what he was doing. He took off his shoe, ripped open the small zipper, snatched the cube and pulled out the capsule.

With his other hand he lifted the cat and flipped it over to cradle it like a baby. He had no trouble stuffing the capsule down the groggy animal's throat and holding its jaws closed. Then he waited for the little cat to swallow. To be sure that the lethal snack was well digested. Richard held it so that its sharp claws could not scratch him. It was a useless precaution: Iggy died without putting up a fight.

Richard was disappointed and laid the cat on the rug. He had expected to play a little longer, that Iggy would be foaming at the mouth, trying to save its life. Instead there was just this dead body lying at his knees.

He grabbed his shoe and felt around in the hiding place where the capsule had been stored. It was empty of course. What had just happened? What was he thinking? What was this madness?

Richard got up and was seized with panic at the idea that the Organization might find out that he no longer had the capsule. But after all, it was a personal possession and the men coming to get him had no reason to suspect anything.

Richard grabbed the corpse by the tail and put it in the sink. He turned the faucet on full blast to wash away any traces of the cyanide that might be sticking to the fur. Then he stuffed Iggy in a garbage bag.

The young man was in a frenzy and could not stop his hands from trembling.

Still, it's not murder. I'll find a good explanation for Susan. As for the Organization, they're not going to shoot me because I lost the capsule.

All of a sudden a loud knock on the door made him jump.

Two days after Richard had left his apartment Anna was back to her normal life, back to her scheduled classes, but all the while thinking of him. He must have arrived in Okinawa by now. Maybe he was already on the base. She went to the library and looked up everything she could find about the archipelago and the American presence on the islands.

Anna carried her dinner tray into the living room and automatically turned on the TV. She had just sat down when the doorbell rang. She glanced at her watch. It was not very late, only 9 pm, and it could be anyone, a colleague, a friend, not necessarily someone from the Organization to come poison her life again.

When she opened the door Anna recognized the girl right away. She was Richard's friend. She looked panic-stricken.

"Sorry to bother you so late," the girl said. "I'm Susan, a friend of Richard."

"Yes, I've seen you before. What can I do for you?"

"Well, look. I just spent two days with my parents and the day before yesterday I left my cat with Richard to take care of him while I was gone."

And Richard left, Anna thought. *It's not the best time to give him a pet. I have to find something to tell this girl to explain why Richard isn't around.*

"And Richard had to go away," she said aloud. "Don't worry. I know about it and I've got the keys. We can both go over there and get your cat. Richard asked

71

me to pick up his mail and make sure everything was okay while he was gone."

"That's not the problem," the girl said. "Me too, I've got keys to his place. I went there this afternoon. His stuff is gone. The room's completely empty and I ran into some guys from a rental agency who were cleaning the place. No, Richard's not coming back. He moved out. Without a word, not even a note. And I'll never find my cat!"

Chapter VI

A big Continental carrier dropped off Richard Tardif at the Okinawa Naha airport at 8 am. The thick fog that covered the island since dawn did not let him enjoy the countryside when landing.

It was Corso—always him—who came to get him the day before to drive him to the Honolulu airport and put him on the plane like a caring father sending his son off to summer camp. All the precautions annoyed the young man who felt like they were treating him as a half-wit who could not take care of himself.

On arriving at Okinawa things were very different. A guy was waiting for him, holding up a sign with the name Richard. This guy apparently did not speak English but he drove fast and very skillfully. They were in the car for over an hour, eating up the miles, and Richard wondered if they would ever get out of the city. The car cruised through huge commercial zones, past long lines of logos, the same as in Hawaii, but dirtier and more squalid.

Richard was surprised to see so many military vehicles on the road. The Americans looked like they were in force on the island of Okinawa.

After a few hours, during which the driver had not uttered a word, the young man finally arrived at his destination. Kuroshio. It was a relatively big town, a city compared to the towns he had passed, and it was cleaner or at least more modern than the places Richard had seen so far on the island. There were a good number of Europeans there and also American soldiers, easily spotted amidst the natives.

The car turned onto a narrow, very steep street that came out in a square high up in the city. An ideal site for a superb panorama of the endless sea.

Then the car pulled up in front of a relatively big building, big enough to have automatic gates that opened slowly as the car approached. His chauffeur, who was still not speaking, parked in an inner courtyard and with a quick nod ordered Richard to get out. He had barely opened the door when a Japanese man, a little more friendly than his travel companion, came up to him in a hurry.

"I'm Cheong Tan. Welcome to Okinawa, Mr. Tarvis."

"Tardif, Richard Tardif," he corrected.

While the driver took charge of his bags, the man signaled Richard to follow him. Mr. Tan was a tall, thin man with graying hair cut very short and dressed in clothes that flowed around his body. He must have been at least 50 years old but elegant and poised. He spoke calmly, with a friendly smile on his face.

"You're leaving tomorrow with my son-in-law. Heading for the island of Kunako. That's where the base is that you have to infiltrate. But for now, rest. Make yourself at home and use the time well before you have to leave."

Dinner was served early, which surprised Richard. Maybe it was a local custom. The young man had no desire to ask questions, so he just sat and watched the chauffeur, transformed into a chef and waiter, filling the table with all kinds of delicacies.

Richard felt like he had shifted into high speed now. No more Corso, no more Ronald with his cheerful laugh. He was dining with a middle-aged Japanese who outclassed all the members of the Organization whom he had met so far.

"You will have to excuse my son-in-law, Mr. Tardif. He couldn't make it this evening. You'll meet him tomorrow at dawn when you leave for Kunako. Help yourself. Those are sea grapes, special seaweed that tastes delicious. It's probably the explanation for the incredible longevity of the inhabitants of this archipelago. Did you know that there are more 100-year old people here than anywhere else in the world, Mr. Tardif?"

Richard shook his head.

"There are also more Americans here than in the rest of Japan. But you already know this. The inhabitants are starting to get fed up with their more and more invasive presence. The Okinawans, however, believe me, are very welcoming, more welcoming than the Japanese. We were hoping that a page in the history of our island would be turned because agreements had to be negotiated between the Japanese and the Americans."

Mr. Tan put down his spoon and turned suddenly very serious.

"Do you know what I think? That our government abandoned us. Despite all the promises it made to the island, the Americans have still not started evacuating their bases and no pressure is coming from Tokyo."

Mr. Tan picked up his spoon again and raised it like a weapon.

"We can only count on ourselves if we want to get anything done. You're Hawaiian, correct, Mr. Tardif?"

"I've lived in Hawaii for a few years."

"Do you know that Okinawa is called the Japanese Hawaii? Our islands have the same average temperature of 75 degrees?"

Richard had never been interested in the average temperature of Hawaii or anywhere else.

"Uh, maybe here there's not the huge waves that you can surf?"

"Aha! Yes, you're right, we don't have the big waves that give you so much fun. But we know other ways to occupy our time."

Richard already regretted his remark. He realized that it was stupid, inappropriate, and he wondered if the response might not have a hidden meaning. He was also hoping that his host would not bore him too much with talk about politics but Mr. Tan skillfully steered the conversation to more mundane topics and the rest of the evening was relaxed and friendly.

Giroja, Mr. Tan's son-in-law, showed up very early in the morning. Richard was all ready and the two of them headed for the small port of Kano where they got on board a speedboat that was big and powerful enough to carry a ton of material.

Giroja had married Mr. Tan's daughter three years ago and he helped his father-in-law by doing all kinds of things. In his thirties, short hair, he was thin but muscular, able to move with graceful agility. Despite his pale skin he was as friendly and smiley as his father-in-law. *No doubt a family tradition,* Richard mused.

After a short, half-hour jaunt, the island took shape on the horizon and slowly as the speedboat got closer to the shore the rugged terrain of Kunako revealed itself to Richard's eyes.

"There are a lot of American bases in Okinawa," Giroja shouted over the sound of the motor on the boat that seemed to be recently built. "But this one is special. The base at Kunako has almost 500 men, a relatively large contingent compared to the other sites. But what's different, too, is that Kunako is tiny. The base takes up practically the whole island. It's surrounded by a jungle where all the bugs come from that we're supposed to exterminate."

"Are they going to search us going in?"

"I don't think so. I've worked there for 15 days already. I've got rid of all the nasty larvae, crawling around in all the pipes. In short, I've done all the dirty work. You just have to finish the job, meaning spray all the rooms, including the basements. Today I'll stay with you to show you the ropes. Tomorrow you're on your own."

Richard nodded and asked, "Is Mr. Tan the one who made the insecticide?"

"My father-in-law is a go-between. He takes care of a lot of things for the islands. The Americans like dealing with him. They trust him. And Mr. Tan likes the Americans. He thinks they're generous, cooperative... totally predictable."

The speedboat took a narrow channel through thick, luscious vegetation. After a few hundred yards the passage roofed with vines and branches seemed to get smaller and smaller and the sky, hidden behind a vault of greenery, disappeared. The air was humid and stuffy, like inside a greenhouse. Richard, who had never seen such dense trees and wild plants, wondered if he might not become claustrophobic and if the land was as hostile everywhere on the island.

They finally came in sight of a more open space where a few crude constructions had been built—a dozen bamboo huts along the bank.

Giroja cut the engine, grabbed a rope and jumped agilely onto the shore. He tied the boat firmly to a big tree and motioned Richard to disembark.

"These huts are empty. They're old fishing cabins dating back to when there were still fishermen on the island. Since the Americans came, everyone here has moved away."

The two men started unloading the material and piling it in one of the huts that looked in decent shape.

"We have an appointment at noon," Giroja looked at his watch. "Which gives us time to have a bite to eat if you want. They'll come get us. The base is around six miles in that direction."

He pointed to a narrow path that seemed to have been cut through the thick vegetation with a machete and lead nowhere in particular.

"This damn jungle," Giroja said, "you'd think it was getting bigger every day. The Yankees have done a hell of a lot of work. They even built a heliport. It's the only way for them to get to the base. At first they tried a landing strip but it was a lost cause. Every day the jungle ate up the runway as if these damn plants had a life of their own."

"And are there dangerous animals in there, carnivores or reptiles…?"

"They're not the most dangerous. If you leave them alone, they won't bother you. No, the worst are the insects. And what you have to watch out for most of all is not to get stung or bit by one of them. If you do, you have to disinfect it right away. Otherwise thousands of bacteria will eat away your skin or your guts. It's the worst thing about this island! That's why the Yankees hide away in their bunker. Moreover, it's the only base in Okinawa where the families of the Marines aren't allowed. See, it's no ordinary base here at Kunako. Let's say that it's more like a camp for army fanatics. GIs on the edge, who love to trudge through the jungle... like superman, right!"

Richard smiled. "So, that's where I'm supposed to do the survey work for a week..."

"Sorry but that's none of my business. I'm here to get you on the base as an employee of Mr. Tan. The rest is your business."

Richard took out his handkerchief and wiped his brow. Late in the morning the heat was already becoming unbearable. The humidity made the air heavier. Richard could understand what Giroja was saying about insect bites: with all this putrid decay infections must spread like wildfire.

Around noon a Jeep driven by a Marine came to get the two men and it headed out for the American base. After a few miles the base appeared out of nowhere.

At first Richard saw only the fences and could not judge the size of the installation. Then his skeptical eyes had to admit the truth: the Marines had accomplished an amazing feat. They had managed to tame the inhospitable jungle and build a huge military complex. Hundreds of buildings stretched into the distance, separated by alleys as wide as boulevards. Behind the barbed wire the men looked like busy ants marching around.

The formalities were kept short. At the guard station Richard just had to show his identity and at the reception desk he handed in the papers that the Organization had provided before he left. Then Giroja introduced Richard to Lieutenant Norton who gave him a vigorous handshake, clearly amused by the young man's amazement.

"There are 432 men here, 9 cooks, 15 civilian employees and one projectionist for the movies."

Richard and Giroja followed the lieutenant as he hurried down the main street.

"You see that hangar-like building?" he halted suddenly and pointed. "That's where the cooks and civilians stay. You'll be with them. We've already cleared space for you. I'll let you set yourself up and take care of your equipment. If you have any questions or problems, don't hesitate to come see me."

The bunk for Richard was in the hangar, a kind of circus tent that just looked like a huge camping tent. Unlike the other barracks the housing for civilians was not made to last.

Giroja explained to the young man what he would have to do, then he left. Richard was alone with all the responsibilities his mission entailed. He had a week to draw up a detailed map of the base.

He started checking his disinfectant equipment. It was strange stuff that reminded him more of a flame-thrower than anything for sanitation purposes.

Anna opened the door of the real estate office and sighed. The first time she had come here was when Richard rented his room and she paid the deposit. She would never have imagined she would be back too soon.

The secretary's explanations brought her face to face with harsh reality: the tenant had definitely left the place and had filled out all the necessary paperwork to terminate his lease. The employee added that he had left the studio spotless and it was rare to find such conscientious, meticulous people.

"But who gave you the keys?" Anna almost shouted.

The secretary obviously had trouble understanding how anyone could be upset when everything was done by the book.

"It was a gentleman, a relative of Mr. Tardif. As I told you, everything's in order. If I remember correctly the gentleman was accompanied by another man who stayed by the door. Anyway, all the papers were signed and for us there was no problem. Don't you worry about the deposit, miss, you'll get it back in two weeks."

"And these gentlemen, did they give you an address?"

"No. We didn't need one because everything was okay. Just a signature."

"Can I see the papers? The signature?"

The secretary was starting to lose her patience and she looked annoyed. "Why? Is there a problem?"

"No, sorry. Drop it. It wouldn't make any difference."

When she left the office in a stupor her eyes were bleary. The truth had just hit her like a ton of bricks: Corso or another, doesn't matter, someone from the Organization had made Richard disappear. He was never coming back to Hawaii.

Anna went home and called Susan to set up a meeting at a fast food joint downtown. The two girls were partners in misfortune. With one slight difference: Anna had a lot more information than Susan about what really happened.

Susan, however, was no idiot and Anna knew it. She knew that for years the youth had been spreading rumors about her in certain neighborhoods. Rumors that luckily were so unbelievable that they never affected her career where nobody would doubt her seriousness or competence. Anna, moreover, was a charming woman and her family, which had lived on the island for generations, had a flawless reputation. The proof: no cop had ever paid her a visit. Plus, Anna was careful and the only ticket she had got for speeding was paid right away.

However, strange events were happening today and things were coming to the surface. Susan eyed Anna suspiciously: this normal-looking, well-behaved professor just might have dragged Richard to his downfall.

Now they were forced to join forces to try to solve the mystery of their friend's disappearance. Anna wanted to team up with Susan. She needed her help but everything concerning the Atomos Organization was taboo. Giving too much information to this girl would be dangerous for her and might even be signing a death sentence for both of them.

"Richard talked a lot about you," Susan was holding a huge hamburger that seemed to defy the law of equilibrium.

"Sometimes he came to my place," Anna explained. "The opposite would have been hard for me. His room was really too small and we don't have the same tastes."

"I think Richard admired you a lot."

"Could be." Anna did not bother to mention that she had paid the deposit for his room and that she had gone by the real estate office in the morning. She went on, "Maybe he decided to change his life. Did he ever say anything like that to you?"

"No, never. And that seems absolutely impossible to me. He wouldn't have taken my cat with him."

Anna recognized how useless this conversation was. The poor girl knew nothing about it. Besides, she suspected that Anna knew more than her, could even feel that the professor was jerking her around. The situation was taking a very bad turn.

"The best thing, if you agree," Anna suggested, "is for each of us to search for him on our own. The first to find a clue to his whereabouts can alert the other. But I'm really afraid that you won't be finding your cat."

"Come on, that's bullshit! He was here two days ago in his messy room with his records and rags lying all over the place. And today it's empty, clean as a hospital, and they're already starting work on it for the new tenant."

Anna nodded slowly without saying a word. She had no miracle answer to give her. "I'll be gone for awhile," she finally said. "I've got a vacation house and some urgent business to take care of. Maybe when I get back there'll be some news. And like I said, each of us can search on our own. Richard only left two days ago and there might be a logical explanation."

When she stood up she realized that Susan had not even mentioned the Atomos Organization. And yet she must have thought that it was the key to the problem. In any case, the communication between them was off from the start. And there was no way to set it straight now.

Richard apparently had not told this girl about going to Okinawa. Susan, therefore, had nothing to do with what was going on. It was absolutely necessary to leave her out of it and out of danger.

The girl looked confused and helpless when Anna left her in front of her double-decker burger, which she had still not taken a bite of.

In the afternoon Anna called the airport to reserve a seat on a flight the next day for the island of Lanai. It was not that she liked the idea but she could not abandon her family heritage to the hands of a criminal organization. Maybe she would find a clue there... Richard had told her he had seen Madame Atomos and talked with her. Could the terrible Japanese woman still be there?

Anna knew that if she wanted an explanation she had to do something.

Even in case of an emergency she had no way of contacting the guys in the Organization and she could go weeks, even months, without a word from them. On the other hand, when they needed her they had no qualms about bothering her at home at any hour of the day or night.

With a bitter smile on her face the young lady sat down at her desk with a pile of papers to correct.

The show on channel 5 was really bad. Anna was watching it only because it reminded her of Richard who loved to watch the presenter. According to him Maila Nurmi had the great advantage of actually resembling a sexy vampire. But Richard's favorite TV host did nothing at all for Anna. She decided to go to bed.

Rather late in the evening, just when she was about to get undressed, the front door bell rang. Anna was hoping at first that it was Corso whose style was to show up at the most inappropriate times as he had done in Anna's apartment. But for once she was hoping it was him because she had questions to ask him that were urgently in need of answers.

But it was not Corso.

This guy did not look very nice either. He was stiff, hollow-cheeked and had a crew cut. He introduced himself as an FBI agent and Anna suddenly felt in terrible danger.

"Are you Anna Bernyanyi? English professor at the Community College?"

"Yes, that's right," she was already wondering if her simple answer might not compromise her safety.

The man stepped inside as if he took her answer for an invitation to enter. "Can you tell me when you were working today, Ms. Bernyanyi?"

She pretended to think a minute. "I stayed home to work today. At noon I had lunch in town."

"With Susan Palmer?"

"Yes, that's right. But apparently you already know this, don't you?"

"I'll get straight to the point, Miss. At the end of the afternoon Susan Palmer was found murdered. We know that you'd seen her a few times."

Anna felt like a wave had crashed over her body. She did not have time to answer or wonder what this guy knew, or what compromising documents he might have in his possession.

The FBI agent continued, "Furthermore, this girl was found in a very nasty state. She'd been tortured with unusual savagery. Unheard-of cruelty. I really wonder whose hands she could have fallen into."

Chapter VII

When the FBI agent left the apartment Anna felt scared to death. Susan had certainly been killed by the Organization. But why tortured? The poor girl did not know anything. They must have followed both of them. And there was a good chance that she was still under surveillance.

The Organization must have thought that Richard had leaked some information or that she had talked to Susan about it. And that was why she was going to suffer the same fate as the poor girl.

Anna realized that, in fact, she only knew the Atomos Organization in a very superficial way. How far were its members capable of going in the name of the fight against American imperialism?

The young lady had deep convictions and because the ideas of the Japanese woman meshed with hers, in part, she had chosen to ignore the methods that the agents of the Organization used. That was the contradiction. By refusing to admit to herself that their acts were criminal she was trying to avoid condemning the battle being fought by Madame Atomos. She had acted like a coward!

Anna was revolted by the proof of her hypocrisy during so many years. All the empty talk about geopolitics with her colleagues also disgusted her... Today she really had no choice. She had to choose sides.

She could go directly to the police and tell them everything she knew. Meaning, basically not much but enough to prevent an act of terrorism in Okinawa.

Her career would be ruined and seeing that she would probably not be thrown into federal prison, she would have to move. Anna did not know what price must be paid by accomplices of the terrorist organization. But one thing was sure: from the Organization there would be no possible redemption.

The face of Jack Corso came to mind. Maybe he would take care of Susan himself? Or would it be one of the guys she had met in her apartment in Honolulu? Or in the house in Lanai?

She remembered that she had a flight booked for the next day. The FBI agent had said that he would come back but he did not tell her to stay in Honolulu. Or maybe she had misunderstood him. Because everything was so mixed up in her head.

The cop had not mentioned Richard. Maybe he was waiting for her to do it. The idea of going first thing in the morning to tell the police everything crossed her mind again, but she decided to take some time to decide.

She would go to the airport and leave for Lanai. A few calm days in her family home would help her see more the situation clearly. There was little chance that she would meet any members of the Organization there. Those people were not constantly invading her life. And even if she did find someone there, it might not be a bad thing: he just might give her some hint about Richard's fate.

But sooner or later she would have to inform the authorities. It was obviously the best way to save Richard. If he was not already dead.

Then she thought of someone else. What was the guy's name she had heard of almost as much as Madame Atomos? Beffort... Smith Beffort. Yes, that was it. Smith Beffort.

The taxi driver had a kind face that Anna had seen before a few times. She felt like she knew everyone on Lanai and likewise was known by everyone who lived here. After all, she had spent her childhood here.

She had never worried about gossip about the comings and goings on the property spreading through the island. The house was pretty remote and helicopters landing in the yard were nothing special in Hawaii where many property owners used this mode of transport for both professional and private matters. And the members of the Organization knew how to be discreet. Moreover, they usually stayed here for only short periods and seldom.

The taxi dropped her off at the gate and she walked up the path that she had taken so many times before as a little girl. As usual the house was empty and spotless.

The first thing she did was open wide the shutters and windows to air it out and let the sun in. Then to exorcise her fears she went down to the basement.

Everything was in order. A magnificent day was in store. Nothing like it to take a break from recent events. When she had time to think about it all, she would call a taxi, go the police station in the town of Kaumalapau and switch sides for good.

Anna slept badly. Nightmares haunted her all night long. She decided to muster all her courage. During the afternoon she called a taxi and was brought to the police station.

She would not mention, directly or indirectly, her membership in the Atomos Organization. Maybe the police in Lanai were in contact with Honolulu; maybe they knew about Susan's murder; maybe she was a suspect, much more serious than she thought... The only way to know for sure was to meet the local police, to tell them what she wanted them to know and to insist on speaking to Smith Beffort for whom she had some information.

In spite of its imposing size the police station in Kaumalapau was shabby. There was a kind of nervousness looming over it, but it seemed to concern only the public, which was fumbling all over the place like extras in an old silent movie. The officers sat around unruffled, concentrating on their administrative tasks.

Anna went up to the desk and asked to see the highest-ranking officer at the station because she had information of the utmost importance to give him. Raising his head slowly from the sports headlines of the local paper the officer on duty stared at her. For a minute he seemed to be sizing her up. *Unless*, Anna wondered, *his brain is still lost in the sports news and he's having a hard time coming back to reality.*

Finally, he picked a phone. "Go sit down," he told her after a few seconds on the line. "We'll call you soon."

She did not have to wait long. Presently she was escorted into an office where a fat man with a moon-shaped face perched on top of a pile of chins welcomed her. The guy, who must have been close to retirement, introduced himself as the chief of police.

"What can I do for you, Miss? You apparently have some very important information to give me?"

From the sarcastic tone he used Anna knew that she was very likely going to be given the boot. She had to do everything she could, however, to be taken seriously. She had just passed the point of no return and there was no turning back.

"Have you heard about the horrible murder in Honolulu yesterday of a girl named Susan Palmer?"

"You know, we don't have a lot of contact with other jurisdictions. There's enough to do on our own island. Why do you ask? Have you come to turn yourself in?"

"Not at all. It's hard enough trying to explain... My name is Anna Bernyanyi. Maybe this name means something to you?"

"You're the Bernyanyi girl!" The chief's face lit up. "Your mother worked at the Bowen's cooperative. The pineapple canneries."

"That's right."

Anna felt like she had just scored a point. Things should go more smoothly now.

"My word, you've become a real lady!" the chief continued. "Do you still live in that pretty house of your parents up in Kaolo Pali? I haven't been in that area in a long time."

I'm glad to hear it, Anna thought, hoping that her reputation from the sketchy neighborhoods in Honolulu had not reached her native island. She had no desire to sully her family's memory.

"I came to see you about a very important matter. So important that I don't know where to start..."

If he tells me to start at the beginning and he thinks he's being clever, I'm up the creek with this guy, she thought.

"Well, start at the beginning," the chief said, a delighted smile spreading across his big, round head.

"I have... or I might have some information about the Atomos Organization that I think might be related to the murder of that poor girl, Susan Palmer. It's pretty complicated to explain. To tell you truth I'd like to meet Smith Beffort."

"Smith Beffort? Is that all, Miss? And you think I can just call him up like that? A simple phone call and he's here?"

"I don't know. I guess so. You're the chief of police and it's important business."

"Maybe, but it has nothing to do with our island. Unless you think the Atomos Organization has infiltrated Lanai?"

Anna did not want to talk about her house. It was a sensitive issue. But she would have to since she had chosen sides with the law. She preferred, however, to wait for Smith Beffort to speak about it.

"In fact, I think that some members of the Organization could be staying on Lanai," she responded.

"Wait a second! You've seen them? You know them?"

"Can you put me on contact with Smith Beffort?" she insisted.

"Maybe. But I have superiors, I have to report, so you have to tell me a little more."

"I can't right now. I even think that starting right now, the moment I walked into this police station, my life is in danger."

"Hold on! Just slow down! You're starting to sound downright paranoid!" the chief almost shouted.

"Still, I'd like you to protect me until I can talk with Smith Beffort."

"Listen, one, you've told me absolutely zilch that convinces me that the Atomos Organization is on Lanai. Two, we don't have enough men for a protective detail. Even if the president landed here in person, I couldn't guarantee his security."

"And if I gave you names?"

"No member of the Atomos Organization is listed with us, Miss. Our island is too small for anything to happen... except growing pineapples, of course."

"So you don't believe me? The names I can provide might not be listed in your station but they certainly are with the FBI."

"If I were you, I wouldn't be so sure, Miss. The members of the Atomos Organization are generally very cagey. Besides, I didn't say I didn't believe you. I just have to be careful, check everything. For now, I advise you to go home. Tomorrow I'll pay you a little visit."

"Why not take care of it right away?"

"I'll tell you one thing that should please you, Miss. Because I can, I have every intention of contacting Smith Beffort as soon as possible. Once that's done, it'll be up to him to decide if he wants to listen to you. The FBI gets loads of information that's bogus, so some preliminary sorting is always necessary. And I suggest that you stay calm. Give me those names you have. I'll arrange a call for you with Beffort and come by to see you in the morning."

"You can't keep me here overnight?"

The chief looked disheartened but he answered firmly, "We can't rightly put you up here in a cell. It's just not done. But there's no reason for you to worry, trust me. Tell me the names and I'll get them to my superiors. We'll contact the FBI and I'll see you tomorrow."

"There's a guy... his name's Corso."

"Corso's his last name... What's his first name?"

"Jack, I think... Yes, it's Jack."

"That's all you have to give me? It's a little vague."

"Look, there are others who might still be on Lanai. Ronald, for example."

"Ronald what? Ronald MacDonald?"

Anna shook her head in discouragement. "Maybe the FBI knows them, chief. It's worth a try at least, especially since I can give you their description."

"If you want," the policeman started writing.

Anna gave him the little information she had. When she was done, the chief looked at the paper full of notes with such exaggerated seriousness that Anna felt even more discouraged. The young lady got up to leave.

"I'll come see you tomorrow for sure, Miss. In the meantime, have a good night and try not to have any nightmares."

Anna was back on the street with a blazing sun beating down in the late afternoon.

Lost in thought, the chief contemplated the paper in his hands. Then he got up and passed by the duty officer.

"I'm going out. Over to Manuel's to get a beer," he stated.

The cop barely nodded his head.

Nobody paid any attention to the chief. He left the building, took a few steps in the direction of Manuel's bar and went into a phone booth on the sidewalk. In spite of the stifling heat in the booth he closed the door tight, picked up the receiver and dialed a number that he apparently knew by heart.

After a few rings a man's voice answered, "Yeah?"

"Is that you, Corso?" the chief said. "We've got a problem. I just had a visit from Anna Bernyanyi. She's becoming a big pain and has to be dealt with right away."

Years ago Richard, too, was a Marine, but the discipline on the Kunako base seemed a lot stricter to him than what he had experienced in his military stint. The guys here were real professionals and the base, because of its geographical position, offered no distractions. The surrounding jungle was an ideal place for obstacle courses and high-level training exercises. In fact, Kunako was more like a prison for army fanatics.

In general, the recruits spent a few months here and left in Olympic shape. Except, of course, for the two percent of poor joes who broke their skulls during the daily exercises.

"Two percent is an average," Peter said.

Peter was one of the civilian personnel. He was the projectionist, responsible for the movies on the base. A private company had provided all the equipment to give a little distraction to the Marines on their nights off.

"They'd do better bringing in whores," Peter grumbled. "Anyway, at night they drink and all they want to see is porn."

Peter was bitter. He was fed up with being stuck on this base where he found life grim. All he wanted was to get back to his native California.

Richard sympathized with him after the first meal in the mess. The soldiers did not mix much with the civilians who were a small minority.

Peter explained that he had inherited the wretched equipment. If he had a projector of 35mm films he would feel like he was working in a real theater, but the pile of French junk he had only ran 16mm and was a disgrace to his calling.

"There are copters that are constantly bringing stuff in. They can transport Jeeps and heavy equipment. They can even drop off tanks to plow through the jungle. But when it comes to bringing in parts for this damn projector that breaks down all the time, no one can do it! There were sailors who mutinied for less! Hey, you know who was in the infirmary the other day? A guy who threw himself out a window. I hope it wasn't because of my films!"

Richard smiled. He had not said a word all evening but sat there listening to the projectionist's monologue. He had spent the day spraying a colorless product on the walls with the device that looked like a flame-thrower. On seeing him at work some soldiers came over and joked about the imitation weapon.

While working he had started reconnoitering in the parts of the base where he could move freely. For the moment he did not take notes. He would see to that later. At present he preferred to commit everything to memory.

"And you, your job, it's to put some invisible gunk on the barracks walls? You figure on doing something else in life or is this what really turns you on?"

"It's a temporary job," Richard answered. "Seasonal work. It's to earn a little pocket change during vacation."

"A little pocket change during vacation? Aren't you a little old for that, man? Me, seasonal workers for me are like... on the farms in California, picking melons or strawberries. Not getting bored shitless in the armpit of the world painting the walls for a bunch of jarheads!"

Suddenly Richard told himself that this guy, with his big mouth, might be a danger. It was the army that needed his services and not a second-rate projectionist with his inappropriate innuendoes to question why he was here.

"Look," Peter went on, "I'm just saying. I know everyone's got to work." He had noticed Richard's annoyed expression and the conversation ended there.

The next day, carrying the equipment on his back, Richard went exploring the far reaches of the base. He walked for a long time along the barbed wire fence that sliced through the thick jungle. Every time he came across a building he entered to spray the insecticide on the walls and in the pipes, all the while forcing himself to memorize the layout. But soon he began to realize how huge the base was and how hard it would be for him to memorize everything.

At noon, during his break, he took out a notepad and scribbled some notes in code so that he would be the only one able to read it. By the end of the afternoon he had made the tour of Kunako.

The following day he would take the same route to jot down a few more details and on the last day he would ask to go into the basements where he was not yet authorized to visit. Still two more days of pretending to kill the pests. Maybe he was really doing it because he did not know the exact nature of the product he was spraying on the walls.

The end of his stay was near. In 48 hours Giroja would come to pick him up. To kill some time Richard decided to go see the projectionist who was battling with his films and projector. A movie was scheduled for the evening but the machine was showing obvious signs of wear and tear. Peter's face was starting to show signs of panic.

All of a sudden someone shouted orders down the corridor, but Peter and Richard, being used to Marine behavior, paid no special attention. Lieutenant Norton, accompanied by five soldiers who did not look very friendly, headed toward Richard.

The officer barked, "Follow us. No questions."

Richard stood dazed for a moment. The Marines brought out their guns and surrounded him.

"What's up with you?" Richard asked. "What's going on?"

Without a word the lieutenant waved him forward. They went straight to the administration buildings. Still escorted by two soldiers who kept their guns on him Richard was shoved into the lieutenant's office.

"Search him," Norton commanded.

The two Marines did as told. The young man was wearing lightweight clothes so the operation was fast. Richard, who had not yet realized the gravity of the situation, tried asking for an explanation.

"You're a spy!" the lieutenant shouted. "You've been caught! I advise you to speak. And double quick!"

What could they have discovered? Richard wondered if this was all a bluff. Nothing in his behavior could have exposed him as working for the Atomos Organization. The information might have come from outside but that was far from certain.

"I don't understand. I don't see what you mean."

Lieutenant Norton gave him a stony stare. "Take him to a cell in bloc 5," he ordered the Marines. "We'll figure out what to do with him later."

Chapter VIII

Anna spent a very long, hard day waiting for the chief. When she started to think of dinner, she lost all hope that he would come.

She was alone in this desperately empty house with only her memories as companions, along with a few objects that she had kept since childhood. A childhood that she had betrayed, just like she had betrayed her parents who would die a second death if they knew that their daughter had entrusted their ancestral home to people like the Atomos Organization.

In the afternoon she had gone out to do some shopping for the few days she planned to spend in Lanai. But she was too anxious and she made up her mind to go back to Honolulu the next day.

She sat down in front of her boiled fish and thought of the chief, how absurd her visit must have seemed, as absurd as every time she had any contact with the police. She and cops did not get along with each other and it always ended in surrealist situations. It was obvious that this guy did not believe a word she said. He and his colleagues would listen to any idle gossip making the round, but when it came to accepting the truth, that was a different matter.

She got up to get a bottle of wine that should have been in the fridge. Anna rarely drank but the last few days called for a little pick-me-up.

On the way to the fridge she glanced out the window into the yard. And she froze. She had seen a figure moving, disappearing behind the trees. At the moment she was not really scared. After all, maybe it was the chief coming to visit her.

Night was gradually falling but there was still some light.

Anna went to the window and looked more closely at what was happening outside. Her blood froze in her veins. There was not only someone in the yard but a car was parked in front with the lights turned off. Ghost-like shadows were moving silently toward her garden path. She did not recognize anyone. It was too dark and they were too sneaky. But one thing was certain: she was in danger.

She ran to the front door and bolted it. Hastily she made a tour of the house to make sure that all the windows were locked. These precautions were useless, she knew. The intruders could just break a window. She needed to close all the shutters but for this she would have to open the windows and she did not want to take the risk. She was now starting to get scared stiff.

She crouched on the floor in a corner of the room and suddenly realized that she had not turned off the light. She was panicking and her actions made no sense.

When she heard the doorbell ring she knew how useless it all was. The members of the Organization just had to ring the bell and she would have to open it.

It rang again. Anna prayed and tried to stay still, tried not to answer the door.

"Open up, Anna. We know you're in there."

She recognized Corso's voice. Her brain refused to connect the sudden arrival of the Organization to her visit to the police, but she had to open the door. She got up like a robot. These people were not used to being disobeyed. Despite the terror that she felt from the nocturnal invasion of her property, she kept a secret hope that the men at her front door were not aware of her talk with the police chief.

"What's going on? What do you want?" her voice trembled through the closed door.

"Open up, Anna!"

Anna's hands were shaking when she started turning the locks. Despite the fear, despite the dread, she could no longer refuse to obey.

She opened the door and the visitors rushed into the house, shoving her aside. Corso was accompanied by two men and an Asian woman. The two men looked vaguely oriental. Anna had never seen them before. But at first sight she knew they were killers. As for the woman, could it possibly be Her? Anna was only a little college professor and she had never crossed paths with Madame Atomos. She was not ready for such an encounter.

She tried to control her fear and sputtered a few words to ask why they were here. Corso punched her in the face. She staggered and fell into a deep, black hole.

After what seemed like an eternity Anna came to. She slowly got her senses back but she did not feel well.

At first she felt like she could not move an inch, could not even shift into a more comfortable position. In fact, she was tied to a chair, her feet and hands tightly bound, becoming number every second. A warm liquid ran down her cheek. Blood, no doubt.

Corso must have hit her very hard. Now she remembered the blow. Her forehead had a nasty gash but oddly she felt no pain. Besides her head, which felt ready to explode, she was not hurt.

What was frightening was that Corso had hit her so hard. What was also frightening was that the three men were now standing in front of her and she was tied to this chair, unable to budge.

The two Oriental henchmen looked preoccupied with something else. Only Corso was watching her, standing a few feet away, strangely silent.

A little farther back the Asian woman was sitting in an armchair and scrutinizing Anna with a look that was both horrified and intrigued. But Anna was sure of it now: this woman was none other than Madame Atomos.

Anna was fully aware of her compromising position. She had spoken to the police. She had gone over to the other side and she had not even imagined that the chief would inform the Organization of her visit and her statement. How could she imagine such a thing in a democracy like the United States?

Anna thought of Susan and her mutilated body. Susan knew nothing and could reveal nothing to anyone. And yet she was killed. Anna had betrayed them. What hope was there for her to get out of this?

Jack Corso looked a little uncomfortable. They had given him a mission and even though he was eager to do it, he still felt awkward when he had to talk about it. He poured himself a glass of alcohol—he must have brought the bottle with him because Anna could not remember having seen it before.

The Japanese woman did not move from the armchair, staring into Anna's eyes. The two thugs were cracking jokes that the young lady did not understand. But despite the blood trickling down her face, despite her fear, the jokes made her relax a little.

"Shut up," Corso barked at the two men. "If you want to joke around, go into the kitchen and get a drink. I'll call you later. For the moment I don't need you."

"We prefer to stay," the bigger of the two replied.

Their faces turned serious and they went and sat near Anna. The tension in the room suddenly skyrocketed.

"We know everything," Corso finally said. "Well, almost everything. Because now you're going to tell us the rest…"

Anna knew at this precise moment that she was going to start screaming. In total panic she could not put two coherent words together.

"You went to the police station to talk to the chief," Corso continued. "And you must have trusted some other people as well. It's a pity because thanks to you we had a nice, quiet little getaway here."

Corso came closer, his face only inches from hers. She could smell the little man's foul, boozy breath. And she could not stop thinking of how Susan was murdered. This whole set-up was not to make her talk. It was her murder they were preparing. Anna did not fear death as much as the torture that was no doubt coming. If she had to be executed, she would rather it be quick. Unfortunately she could not reach the cyanide capsule that the Organization had been kind enough to give her.

"But whatever you might have said," Corso went on, "we can't take any chances. We have to give up this charming house for good. You understand what that means? You're going to be put to death. You won't be the first and certainly not the last."

Anna wondered what a bullet felt like entering the body. Corso and his sidekicks must be professionals and the work would be done cleanly. This thought did not keep her from trembling. She also wondered what miracle was stopping her from screaming.

The little man ran his finger delicately down Anna's bloody face. When he took it away, there was blood dripping off it. Corso took a handkerchief out of his pocket and wiped his finger carefully. Then he nodded to the two men who jumped up. They grabbed her and held her tightly, to keep her even more firmly glued to the chair.

There was something wrong here. Things were not supposed to happen like this. She was breathing in the animal scent of the two goons and feeling their strong paws on her shoulders. Then she started screaming bloody terror.

The man who was on her left let her go and turned slightly to face Anna. He gave her a resounding slap, then another. The blows only increased the terror she felt and she screamed more loudly.

Anna no longer felt anything. Her whole body was groaning but she felt no pain. Only dull thuds booming in her head. She could not see very well what was happening in front of her. Her vision became blurry.

Then she stopped screaming. The blows stopped raining down and she felt a dull pain slowly invade her body. A red veil was slowly drawn over her eyes but she remained conscious and heard but did not really understand what her torturers were saying. They were probably talking about bashing and trashing her to make their pleasure last.

Another hard slap knocked her unconscious.

For a long time, without dreams, without sight, Anna fell into a blessed black hole where she could curl up in the depths of her mind. Time was suspended and her suffering and her fear dwindled away.

But an awful pain suddenly drilled into her head and forced her to come back to reality. A pain that shot up from her hand through the nerves in her right arm.

One of the guys had slipped the blade of a knife under one of her fingernails and then stabbed it into her flesh.

The pain was unbearable. Anna was praying for death as soon as possible and was sorry that she had nothing to confess. The only thing on her mind was putting an end to the atrocious suffering.

She heard Corso's voice in a fog.

"You understand, we have to make an example of you. When the police find your corpse, they'll know that the Atomos Organization is pitiless. It'll prove to the Americans that we're not joking around if we need to torture you like this. The Yankees love all these stories about Japanese torture. We also have to set an example for the people who do our menial work. Natives here are always ready to do anything for a bag of cash but they can't help talking about it afterward. So, we're forced to step in and shut them up."

The pain in her hand was slowly letting up. Her index finger was covered in blood so she could not tell if the nail was completely torn off.

"When the cops find your corpse, they'll be horrified at the sight. We've stored a little equipment in your basement that you don't even know about. They're everyday objects, completely harmless, but with a little cleverness they can cause frightful damage to the human body. Do you remember Lola, dear Anna?"

Anna remembered nothing and did not answer. She only wanted to faint again and find a little relief. Corso left the room and went to the stairs leading to the basement. Little by little the memory of Lola came back to Anna's mind. Lola was a local bird that she kept as a child. The bird died a long time ago, nothing was left except the empty cage that had been put in storage.

Corso was back, carrying the cage. Through the bloody veil that obscured her vision Anna recognized it. There were small metal bars covered with light green paint that was flaking away. There was also another color that would have made the young lady jump if she had enough energy to move.

"I'll explain it to you briefly," Corso said. "I know you're in no condition to understand very technical details but you'll get the gist."

The little man brought the cage up to Anna's face and in a pompous tone launched into a kind of lecture.

"Maybe you don't see where you're at, but this cage has been completely modified. It was Kanoto Yoshimuta's idea. You know that's the real name of Madame Atomos. She explained to me the origin of this torture. I can't remember exactly what she said but what I'm sure of is that it was not originally a Japanese torture, which she's probably sorry about. But in brief, Madame Atomos' big idea is to modify things. This extraordinary woman is capable of transforming the secret underground bases in the US. She is smarter than the best Yankee scientists but she also takes great pleasure in cleverly transforming the most ordinary objects. It's a kind of hobby, if you will."

While concentrating on his explanations Corso slowly pivoted the cage in his hands.

"This cage, as you know, was meant to keep one or two birds. But look closely. We made the opening big enough to fit a human head. It's also been separated into two parts, the second can fit a big rat. A trap door can be opened between the two. Once the rat is free, the rodent will be right in front of your face and it'll gnaw away, slowly, carefully. It may not be terribly original but you have to admit that Madame Atomos knows her classics.

Me too. Like every man brought up on Huxley and his novel <u>Brave New World</u> where this abominable torture is described in detail. The genius idea is to have transformed a simple birdcage into a torture cage."

It's not in Huxley, you stupid jerk, Anna mumbled in her head. *It's not Huxley, you creep! You loser...*

She could not move. She did not try to fight when the two guys put her head inside the cage that had once housed her island bird. The system of holding her neck was very sophisticated: they could seal it tight without damaging the skin.

Anna's eyes were now in front of a grill that made her feel like she was inside a miniature theater. The second part of the cage was still empty. But Anna could feel her breathing speed up.

Through the bars of the cage she could barely see what the guys were doing. On the other side of the room Corso and one of them were busy with something. Then suddenly she noticed little red spots stuck to the metal bars. She turned away and focused on the Asian woman who had not moved for a long time.

And then it was the horror!

She was not expecting this. Well, not so quickly. She had not seen it coming.

The monster was thrown into the cage and landed a few inches from her face. This huge mass. This stink and these shrieks. Right in front of her. This foul animal spinning around. Its weight and flurry of activity shaking the cage that the torturers were forced to hold still.

Then the rat's eyes saw Anna's and the dirty beast launched itself at the grill separating them. Anna had never seen such a big rat. But this was the first time she had seen one so close. The two men had trouble keeping the cage straight, jolted as it was by the frenzied lurching of the animal.

"We're going to make an agreement, the two of us," Corso suddenly spoke up. "As long as you don't scream and you keep your mouth shut, we won't open the trap door and let the rat out. Of course, it's only postponing the inevitable. We have every intention of killing you in the most gruesome way possible, but you can put it off for a few minutes."

It's not Huxley, she repeated mentally, as if clinging to a rational thought.

"To pass the time, I'll explain to you how your friend died. You know, the girl in Honolulu, who you told about us, who we had to eliminate. Well, this is the same rat that killed her. But in a different way. Because in Honolulu we didn't have a cage like this."

This time Anna made a superhuman effort not to scream. She wondered how long it would take for the animal to tear off her face. There was also the possibility that all this was just a bluff. Just a macabre game to teach her a lesson.

"We lay the girl down naked on her bed," the little man continued. "Pretty thing, by the way. And then we put the rat in a metal bucket and turned it over, holding it down on the chick's belly. At first she just got her belly button nibbled. I'd say she wasn't relaxed enough to appreciate what a fit of laughter could do to some people. Generally, anybody who busts up laughing in such circumstances sinks fast into madness."

Corso looked at the goons holding the cage.

"The former tenant of this cage was called Lola and it was a bird. I see we haven't given a name to its new occupant."

The rat had stopped moving in the corner. The smell of blood trickling down Anna's face had excited it at first but it seemed to realize that it could do nothing about it for the moment. And it was calm.

"So, let me finish my story. The girl wasn't laughing, of course. We were forced to gag her so we wouldn't bother the neighbors and could function in peace. We started heating up the bucket with the rat inside. It got more and more uncomfortable and started trying to find a way out. The metal was too hard for its teeth to bite through. So, there was only one possibility left: go at the soft belly flesh of your friend. The rat started with the belly button and went all the way up to the windpipe. A kind of tracheotomy of sorts."

Corso's index finger was tapping the small lever that activated the trap door.

"I see you're very brave. "You haven't uttered a single peep and that gives you the right to a little more delay."

It wasn't Huxley, asshole, she held onto this thought with all her strength.

She was trying to imagine something else to cling to when the noise of a stampede crashed through the room. She heard gunshots. But the rat and its bristling fur blocked her view.

Something was happening. The two guys seemed to have disappeared.

Anna was still tied to the chair and wearing the abominable helmet. But the situation was turning. The shadows in the corner of her eyes were no longer the same. Even though her field of vision was small, Anna spied Corso pulling out his gun and slipping behind her. He was the one holding the cage now.

The Japanese woman had disappeared and the rat was more excited than ever.

"Lower your weapons!" Corso shouted, "or else the girl will lose her face in two seconds."

Some men had entered the room. Maybe the police. Or the FBI. There were three of them, one of them Asian who seemed to be their chief.

Anna was not very sure but she thought that Corso's two accomplices were lying face down on the ground.

In spite of the gun he held, Corso was in a bad position. The young lady feared that he would shoot her in the head before being gunned down, but she saw his little finger was still playing with the trapdoor lever. Even if he opened the grill the police would have plenty of time to save her before the rat chewed off her face. The low-life seemed to care more about the rat than his own life.

"Hands in the air!" the Asian ordered. "I'm Yosho Akamatsu, special agent of the Tokkoka, Japanese police."

"And that gives you the right to bust in here and…" Corso began. But he did not finish. One of the two men with the Asian cop had just put a bullet in his head. Corso collapsed. The wobbly cage toppled over and the grill suddenly shot open. Anna was instantly facing the rat with no protection. Terrified, she threw her head back. The animal slid and bumped into her face. In a panic and excited by the smell of blood it started to bite off a piece of her left cheek.

The three men ran to help her. Yosho Akamatsu fumbled with the complicated latch at the base the neck but Anna howled in pain and struggled with all her might, which only made his job harder.

"Hold her still!" the Japanese yelled. "Try not to move, Miss."

And yet the rat went berserk with all the commotion. It planted its sharp teeth into Anna's face as her cries of pain became louder and shriller.

Yosho Akamatsu saw that he was not going to free her like this. He took his revolver and shot the animal at point blank range. The bullet exploded the body that twitched for a few seconds before it lay still forever.

Anna had crumbled, too. She had stopped screaming. Only a muted whimper escaped her lips.

The three police officers leaned over her and finally got the infernal helmet off her head.

Chapter IX

Agent Yosho Akamatsu was leaving Queen's Hospital Center in Honolulu. He had not stayed long, just long enough to get news of Anna Bernyanyi and make sure that she did not need any extra protection.

The young woman was safe and sound but even with the work of the best surgeons her face would be scarred for life.

Lying almost unconscious on the hospital bed, she was far from suspecting that the intervention of the Japanese police was anything but the result of an investigation that had started days ago, in the archipelago of Okinawa. After events that were so astonishing that they could have been caused by none other than the Atomos Organization. But they had not claimed responsibility.

Most of what happened in the space of a few days had remained secret, a tight lid being kept on all information. But these events took place on several bases in Okinawa where entire families of soldiers were living and they talked to friends and relatives on the American continent. A few telephone conversations and leaks were inevitable.

Yosho Akamatsu headed for the HPD (Honolulu Police Department) and called agent Smith Beffort who was still in Okinawa.

"We were wrong," the Japanese said. "This trail led us straight to a branch of the Atomos Organization. But right now we've hit a roadblock. Three guys are dead and the girl who had to be hospitalized can't talk. There's still the kid's mother who's being guarded at the

111

police station but she can't be held long since we've got nothing on her."

"The kid? You mean Richard Tardif?" Beffort asked.

"The same. Thanks to him we followed the leads and that's why I flew over to Hawaii. But I have to admit that I'm stuck and this affair seems more and more complicated."

"Maybe, but at least we're sure now that what's happened over the last few days is really the work of Madame Atomos."

"Indeed, it seems likely to me."

"Keep it going on your side. Your investigation is certainly not finished. As for me, I'm afraid it hasn't even started."

Beffort slammed the phone down. Not out of rudeness but his mind was elsewhere.

He had landed in Okinawa the day before. His boss, Jonathan Forbes, had sent him because, as he said, "Only Madame Atomos could be at the heart of recent events."

Smith Beffort was very tempted to believe him. Even if the events in question had not been claimed by the fearsome Japanese woman, they had all her markings, the FBI agent was sure of it.

Therefore, he arrived in Okinawa the day before on board a military plane specially chartered to take him to Okuma, one of the 15 American bases set up on the Japanese islands. The biggest and most central, which was in downtown Okinawa, had lost every single one of its troops in one night. At dawn it was a ghost base.

"You understand," General Bixby had told Beffort, "that it's going to be very hard for us to keep this secret.

Even more so since the Okinawa base is not the only one to suffer disaster."

"How many other bases were affected?" Beffort asked him.

"As far as I can say right now, three. But things are moving fast. It's all brand new. See, we're in the eye of the hurricane and we could end up disappearing in the same way at any moment."

Beffort, however, was more cautious. "I have to admit, General, that given the information I've got, I can't say for sure that this has anything to do with the Atomos Organization."

"What's more," General Bixby resumed, "when I say three other bases were affected, it's not exactly right. Truth is that the soldiers vanished in the three camps but in the third they reappeared."

"Alive?"

"No, all dead, Mr. Beffort. All dead. But that's not the worst of it."

"What could be worse?"

"It's why I asked for your collaboration. Only the mark of Madame Atomos could be worse than death."

"I don't follow you, General. Could I see one of these Marines? Where are the bodies?"

"Some of them have been brought here. You can judge for yourself."

General Bixby brought the FBI agent to the infirmary on the base. Thanks to his profession Smith Beffort had often visited sites that had witnessed violent events. Generally there was feverish activity around. But here he noticed an oppressive silence. The Marines, all ranks of soldiers, were obviously in shock.

"I'd rather you see it with your own eyes, otherwise they'd never believe me in Washington," the General mentioned.

Beffort entered the infirmary, a small room but immaculately clean. He was expecting a kind of funerary chapel where the remains would be lined up solemnly. But nothing of the sort.

Puzzled, he looked questioningly at the general. The officer pointed to a table in the middle of the room. Small bundles of white linen were lying on it. Beffort picked one up and carefully unwrapped it.

It's a cat skeleton, he wanted to shout, but he said nothing and ran his fingers over the animal's white bones. The agent's rational brain was having a hard time admitting that this was in reality a miniature human skeleton.

"It's a fake skeleton," he finally uttered.

"We've done every possible test. What you're looking at is a real human skeleton, maybe eight inches tall. It's the same for the 234 others found on the Okuma base."

The FBI agent kept silent.

"You see that we didn't call you here for nothing," the General added.

"It's unbelievable!" Beffort exclaimed. "I can't believe it right now. Maybe later… but no, impossible. If Madame Atomos is behind this, it's no doubt a trick, a hoax…"

At regular intervals Marines came into the infirmary in total silence. Protocol seems to have been laid aside. The men whispered to each other. The general jotted down what they told him and gave orders with restraint and patience.

Smith Beffort examined what looked like a macabre joke. "Do you have more information... I mean... something more reasonable to give me, General?"

"Certainly. We came across an important clue that led us to Mr. Tan. He's a native of the islands. An influential guy who already has a little reputation, a reputation suspicious enough for the Japanese authorities to be watching him closely. It would've put him in the midst of all kinds of trafficking. But well, you know how the Japanese thumb their nose at American soldiers, Beffort. For them, with all our bases stuck all over Okinawa, we're pretty much occupying their territory."

"I guess recent events might change the stakes..."

"Exactly right, Beffort. The Japanese, therefore, decided to help us. You never know, if by chance there weren't just American soldiers who were disappearing! We had access to confidential information about the traffic in arms where Mr. Tan was involved but along with some of our soldiers."

"Okay. But I don't see the relation to this affair."

"Of course not. Just hold on. Listen, last week Mr. Tan had provided a few of our bases with maintenance personnel. For some bug extermination or something like that... And it happened that on two of these bases the maintenance men in question were acting suspiciously and they found a weird device in their equipment that looked a lot like a bomb."

"Oh, now it gets interesting."

"In fact, these 'bombs' didn't explode. The thing was that right when they started to examine them, they literally disintegrated. And so we still don't know what they really were or what they were supposed to be used for."

"You interrogated the maintenance men?"

"One of them killed himself by swallowing a cyanide capsule. The second didn't have one on him. He's being held prisoner on the island of Kunako. He's a young man by the name of Richard Tardif. He says he didn't know he was carrying anything in his stuff. He claims he's being set up."

"Watch out that he doesn't find another way to kill himself and be careful that he doesn't escape. I want to interrogate him. The devices brought onto the bases might very well be the cause of the grisly phenomenon. We absolutely have to make all these people talk."

"Regarding Mr. Tan, that might be tough. He's taken off, just like his daughter and son-in-law. The Japanese cops are looking into it but we shouldn't expect too much from them. Collaboration has its limits."

"When it comes to Madame Atomos there are no limits. Do you know where this maintenance worker came from?"

"He's an American recruited from Hawaii. That's all I know right now."

"Okay. I'll get my colleague and friend Yosho Akamatsu on the case and you'll see what a real American-Japanese collaboration can do. One thing is sure: this guy Tardif, there's no way we can let him escape from Kunako before he's told us what he knows."

It was after this meeting with General Bixby that Beffort asked Akamatsu to rush over to Honolulu and investigate Richard Tardif's circle.

Important work had been undertaken at the Bhuto base. This had forced the military families to relocate temporarily outside the base. For three months they had been housed in comfortable hotels downtown. The soldiers' wives were obligated to get used to all kinds of inconveniences. Eve Newman was one of them.

Eve and Alan still had no children, which was just as well since Alan was assigned to Okinawa. They were supposed to return to the US in less than a month. They could see the end of the tunnel.

Life on the islands was not so bad as long as you ignored the nasty fish stew that constantly molested your sense of smell. Living outside the base forced Eve to ingest all the food that she could never even stand the smell of. But since the day before things had changed. Something serious was happening on the base and the worst of it was the lack of information.

All the wives suffered from the anxiety, even panic, that surrounded the base as if events out of anyone's control were unfolding inside. At first they forbid them to enter the base and then the women were not allowed to even communicate with their husbands.

But all this happened very fast and straightaway the military authorities were unable to quiet the rumors. The craziest ones said that the Marines had all disappeared and the base was completely empty. They also said that three soldiers had miraculously escaped but nobody could say why. Everyone had their own ideas.

The officials, however, admitted quickly enough that the wives of the soldiers who were presumed vanished, had the right to know. The restrictions were partly lifted, which was not so hard since the Bhuto base was in upheaval and everyone was busy with their many, different tasks.

The wives of the Marines decided to move back onto the base without anyone thinking of posing a formal opposition. The military authorities warned them, of course, that the phenomenon could happened again at any moment and that it could be dangerous for them and their children. But nobody forbid them outright from coming back to live at the site of the disaster.

Eve Newman, therefore, went back to the housing unit where she and Alan lived. Everyone was in shock. The women were wandering through the empty buildings among the soldiers dispatched to the site to look for clues. All of them displayed the same confusion, the same desolate face.

There were also children, some of them very young, and the Bhuto base started to look like a huge nursery.

The first night passed in an eerie, almost unreal silence.

The next day was spent organizing logistics and supplies. And always the same question: "Should we really stay here?"

"I'm going to ask to go back to the US," one of the woman confessed. The others preferred to wait a little while.

Eve was torn. She was convinced that Alan, like the other Marines, was not dead. They had disappeared but there was nothing to prove they were killed.

On the second night Eve could not get to sleep. She left her apartment around midnight. The air was fresh. In spite of all the anxiety the base was silent. Eve heard only the sounds of the city that gave a semblance of life to the dreary place. The moon was almost full. It was a perfect time for meditation. Eve looked into the sky and thought of Alan.

"You can't be up there, my dear. Not yet."

On saying this she surprised herself by realizing that she believed it. In truth, since she had heard the news, she had never stopped hoping. For her, her husband was simply absent.

She heard someone call her name. It was Ruth, one of her friends. Well, one of the military wives who she got along with better than others. She was leaving a building and Eve saw her come out of the darkness.

"Come quick!" Ruth cried. "Something's happening!"

Inside the building a Marine took Eve into a room where other women were sitting around, visibly shocked.

"Has Alan come back?" she asked. "Is he dead? Did you find him?"

"It's not that," the soldier answered, looking as defeated as the women present. "Something weird's been going on all evening."

"Have you seen my husband?"

"Take it easy, Mrs. Newman. We can't say we've really seen your husband."

"They're ghosts," one of the women explained, her whole body trembling. "The ghosts of our husbands are wandering around the building. My God, they've been killed and they're coming back to haunt these walls!"

"What? What's all this madness about?" Eve asked the Marine.

"I have to admit that it's troubling... Some kind of ectoplasm. Vague shapes that materialize and then disappear. We've recognized the soldiers from the base. But they're only shadows forming around us."

"And is my husband one of these shadows?"

"Among others, yes. They're all here. Everyone who worked on the base."

"Where are they? Come on, show me!" Eve yelled in a voice bordering on hysteria. She had grabbed the soldier's jacket and was on the verge of tears.

Gently the Marine removed her hand and motioned her to follow him. All the women got up and the small group headed for the mess hall. The soldier opened the door.

Eve had heard of spirit materialization. She and Alan had even participated once in a séance but neither of them really believed in it. So, she was totally unprepared for what she was about to see.

A ballet of human shadows floating in the mess hall. 100 hazy forms drifting three feet off the ground. Some went right up to the ceiling only to drop straight back down and crawl over the floor. Others just vanished into a wall and popped back out an instant later.

"We have to call an exorcist," one of the women said.

Oddly, Eve was not scared. There was nothing frightening about this extraordinary vision. On the contrary, the ectoplasms, if you could call them this, were emitting a kind of intense glow. A mix of bright colors swirling in space.

Sometimes one of the bodies brushed by Eve, then swung away in a kind of perpetual whirlwind. The young lady tried to find Alan among the shadows, but her husband was not there. Besides, the ectoplasms did not seem to acknowledge the groups of wives as they continued their spooky waltz.

"Do you think you saw Alan?" she asked the Marine.

"He was here a little while ago, then he left. If you look closely you can recognize some of the others."

Indeed, Eve spotted a few acquaintances among the fleeting, fuzzy faces.

"What do you think it is? In your opinion, is it some top-secret military experiment? Holograms or something like that?" she asked the Marine.

"No, I don't think it's an army experiment. A secret trial that went wrong is pretty unlikely, I think. Ghosts could explain it. The only problem is that I don't believe in ghosts."

Other soldiers gradually joined the group that was gathering inside the mess. Other wives showed up too. Soon the room was full of people.

It looked like a New Year's Eve Ball except that there was no noise. The apparitions moved around in total silence and the few people who spoke did so in whispers.

One of the shadows suddenly hovered next to Eve. A blurry apparition without any definite outlines. What the young lady would formerly have called a ghost. But this ghost was her husband. Eve could clearly see Alan's features in the spectral face. And the joy of finding him was quickly replaced with worry. Because of the look in his eyes.

The shadow of the man who had been her husband was flitting around her. And yet now that she had recognized him, she was trying at all costs not to look into his eyes. Unfortunately, this was not easy.

In a short time Eve felt a rush of unpleasant emotions wash over her. She did not understand but one thing was obvious: she could not stay in this room. Her heart was racing. Adrenaline was surging through her veins.

The door of the mess was wide-open and only 15 feet away. She started to back away toward the door. The other women stepped aside and Eve noticed that she had suddenly become the center of attention. She held back screams. So as not to panic even more. She had to leave calmly, escape from the look in the ghost's eyes.

She kept her eyes on the ground and tried to concentrate on something else, step by step, retreating. Farther away from the group she shook free of Alan's hold, not feeling him around her anymore. He must have gone into the weird dance that looked like it would never stop.

What had happened when she met his gaze? The wonder turned to terror. The surprise transformed into a nightmare.

She finally got out the door as the newcomers were pushing their way inside. She was pushed and shoved aside and had to hold onto the doorjamb before she ended up crouching in a corner of the corridor.

Eve was taking deep breaths to calm the wild beating of her heart and try to control her emotions. That was when she looked up and understood her mistake.

Alan, or someone else, had not left her and was still dancing around her. This time she could not look away.

Her heart was still beating too fast. It did not have enough time to return to normal.

What she saw in Alan's eyes was something she would never be able to describe.

A dreadful howl echoed through the walls of the whole building. The Marines and the women in the mess came running.

She was taken immediately to the infirmary but the soldiers and the women who saw her leave knew that it was too late. One look at the unbearably deformed expression of horror on her face was enough.

Chapter X

After Lieutenant Norton broke into the projection room with his men, things got hot and hurried on the Kunako base.

Everything had started with finding amidst the extermination material that Richard Tardif was using a small cylinder that they first thought was a bomb. While ten soldiers were examining it the cylinder disappeared in a flash or rather it disintegrated in a split second.

But this second event was completely unknown to Richard, sitting alone in a cell as he was.

Some guys came to interrogate him. Lieutenant Norton came too and several times. Every time his questions were short and brutal. However, to Richard's great surprise the violence was only verbal. At no moment was he ever physically molested.

Without any outside information Richard knew nothing about what was really happening.

On his side the lieutenant got the most surprising news. Surprising, confusing and contradictory. They were informing him about the extraordinary events taking place on other bases in Okinawa and they confirmed that the Atomos Organization was no doubt involved.

Then, before he had time to digest this news, the officer was made aware of another event, just as incredible, that happened on one of the bases. Everything was happening way too fast for sure.

"Watch your prisoner closely," a phone call from the top of the military hierarchy ordered him. "Make him talk but be sure he can't give you the slip or give himself a death sentence. Smith Beffort the FBI agent arrived in person in Okinawa and he'll come to interrogate the suspect shortly. For the moment we're too busy with what's happening on the other bases but we'll be coming to pay you a visit soon."

Being a good soldier the lieutenant obeyed. But he did not really see how a prisoner could escape from Kunako.

They had found no weapons on Tardif and everything that might be used for suicide was taken away. He was taken to a cell that he was not about to escape from. The camp, it was true, was not built to house prisoners, but Richard had been shut up in a storeroom where he was handcuffed on his wrists and ankles. Therefore, there was no risk of him escaping.

When he saw the young man chained up like this Peter shouted at the soldiers, "Don't you think you've gone a little too far?"

The projectionist had been authorized to visit Richard. The two men had got along and Lieutenant Norton figured that Peter might be able to get some information out of him. At first Richard was as surprised as Peter but he quickly understood that he was being used and manipulated. The Atomos Organization did not care a rat's ass about him!

The Atomos Organization! Good God, just thinking about it sent shivers down his spine.

Okay, it was true, by losing the cyanide capsule he had not followed orders to the letter. Right now he should be dead.

Richard far preferred to be in the hands of the American military than in those of the Organization who surely had no desire to spare him. Here at least he had a chance to keep on living.

He asked Peter to get the lieutenant and said he was ready to cooperate.

"I've been set up," he explained to the officer when he came into his cell. "I was just told to make a map of the place. I didn't know that my equipment was tampered with."

"You know you can be court martialed."

Richard did not really know what this meant. Just like his involvement with the Atomos Organization, the death penalty was too abstract for him. The young man could not gauge the importance of his actions and he thought there were enough extenuating circumstances for the American army and maybe the justice system to go easy on him.

"I want to help you," he continued. "But I think I've already told you everything I know. For the moment I don't see what else I can say."

"And this cylinder with your equipment?"

"I don't know. I was totally set up, I told you."

The lieutenant did not push him. Obviously the prisoner knew nothing about the cylinder that had disintegrated. The kid sounded sincere. But orders were orders.

"We have to keep you locked up until the people who will decide your fate get here."

"Can't you take the cuffs off? It's like being on a slave ship."

"Sorry. We can't do anything for you right now. The Kanuko base wasn't designed to keep prisoners. We have to make do with what we've got on hand. Anyway, I don't think you'll have to wait long."

The lieutenant approached the prisoner.

"Do you know that Smith Beffort is coming in person to interrogate you?"

Smith Beffort! The name rang a bell in Richard's head. Smith Beffort, the famous FBI agent, the sworn enemy of Madame Atomos, was coming to interrogate him.

The young man felt like he had become a VIP. If only Anna was here to see this! But a shiver ran through his whole body. If Smith Beffort wanted to talk to him, it meant that things were more serious than he thought.

The lieutenant left the cell and the prisoner under the watch of a soldier.

Information from the other American bases was waiting for him in his office. Each piece of news was crazier than the last.

On the Bhuto base all the soldiers had disappeared and they found their 8-inch skeletons.

The Lieutenant got a call from the General Staff. They asked him if there were any sudden disappearances at Kunako or other strange incidents. He answered that nothing so far had been noticed.

Richard would have liked to get a good sleep before the next interrogation but all he could do was doze in fits and starts like being sick. The only positive thing was that his wrists and ankles no long hurt. His belly, however, was acting up: his guts were cramping and his stomach started to hurt.

The soldier guarding him looked in a bad way also. The Marine was clenching his jaw. With his hand on his belly he seemed to be suffering the same symptoms as Richard, who was curled up on the floor.

The prisoner looked at him and said, "We must have eaten something bad. I've got a stomachache too. Maybe we should do something about it."

The Marine did not respond. Richard could see that the soldier was in serious pain. It looked like he got the worst of it.

"Go to the infirmary, man. You can leave me alone for five minutes." Richard got up and dragging his chains behind him he was going to approach the soldier. But all of a sudden, as unbelievable as it might seem, he had to face the facts: his wrists and ankles were not as tight as before. There was a little play now between the metal and his skin. The handcuffs could even slip easily up his forearm. It did not take much effort to move more freely.

The surprise gave way to joy, although tempered by the growing pain in his belly and by an awful migraine that started drilling his head.

Richard glanced at the soldier. The poor guy was now face down on the ground, holding his stomach and writhing in pain. He was suffering too much to worry about what his prisoner was doing.

With one strong pull Richard managed to free his hands from the steel bracelets. Then he went at his ankles. In no time at all he was free. He took the keys from the Marine's pocket, who could think about nothing but his tormented belly, and a few seconds later he was out of his cell.

He ran fast down the corridor when his own pain let up a little and gave him enough respite to think and move. He had to find a way out. Out of the building and then off the base and finally off the island of Kunako and away from Okinawa! A huge program…

Outside the building the soldiers were in full panic. Men were running all over the place. Some Marines, clearly in the grips of immense pain, were rolling on the ground; others were less affected—at least they managed to stay on their feet—but were pale and moaning.

In the midst of this chaos Richard was hoping he could pass unnoticed.

Instinctively he headed for the building where he had stayed on his arrival. Alarmed soldiers were pouring out of the barracks. A droning wail came out of the mouths of all the men in agony. As Richard snuck around the base he saw the number of Marines lying on the ground, some of them completely still, multiply.

He, too, on his left side felt again a stabbing pain from his lower back up through his chest. Like it was gnawing away at his guts. Like something was altering his body. But maybe this was just his impression.

He kept moving. He could not see very clearly what was happening around him. His eyes were starting to act up. Impaired vision, in fact. Good God, what was happening to him?

Now it seemed impossible for him to reach the room, which was somewhere too far away. Like a robot he headed for the big, gray, prefabricated building that he recognized. The kitchens! Richard went in, feeling an unexplainable sense of relief. Inside there were shadows stumbling around and he, too, was forced to lean against the wall to keep from falling backward. The pain was becoming more and more intense.

All of a sudden he was in front of the door leading in the cold-storage room. He knew the place. A few days earlier they had told him not to deal with it right away because the huge refrigerator held all the meat needed to feed the men for several days. They had asked him to wait to spray it.

He remembered that they had told him that the temperature reached -20. Maybe the cold would help, would

kill the microbes or bacteria that were in his body or...
maybe it would kill him. But it was worth a try. Anyway, he had no choice.

He grabbed the silvery handle of the cold room. The
icy temperature gave him a little relief right away, so he
shut the heavy door behind him. He was in a vast refrigerator, among huge slabs of meat and all kinds of fowl.
Suddenly he felt better. Numb but a lot better.

If he stayed here he would freeze but he had no desire to leave. If he had to die, he preferred a suicide here.
He sat down in a corner and waited.

For more than three hours Naoto waited in his small
apartment in the suburbs of Kyoda. It was always the
same thing with the American soldiers. True she did not
expect much, no more than she expected anything from
men in general. But this one, he could have made a little
effort. Especially since she had been feeling that her relationship with this guy was settling down. Relatively
speaking, of course, since Marines always end up going
back home.

With Adam, however, it might have been different.
They had something in common: Naoto was an artist and
Adam liked her work a lot. Or else he was just pretending in order to sleep with her, who knows... She was
really starting to question this seriously, even more so
since this was not the first time he had stood her up.

Naoto told herself that it would better to forget all
about this evening that she had planned to be romantic.
She had made French fries and bought ketchup because
she knew Adam liked this. He also loved the cheese-
burgers that were sold a dozen to the box at old Kwong's
grocery store. On the other hand, Adam hated fish stew
and all the local food. He had even become violent one

night when she had lovingly cooked a dish of stuffed crab and sea grapes. They had almost broken up that night before Naoto went out to buy a six-pack of beer.

Since her boyfriend was still not there Naoto decided to continue working on her sculpture. She worked in all kinds of material, in fact whatever she could find and could stimulate her inspiration. She loved to sculpt the fanciful animals of Japanese mythology. Animals so weird that one day, standing in front of her work, Adam had asked her if she was on drugs. She laughed. Adam was so funny!

Lately, she was working on a figurine in clay and glass that had to be made 20 inches tall and that she was starting to be very proud of. Naoto realized that the longer she worked, the more original and interesting her creations were. She thought that her talent just might be recognized some day.

She had just started on the work when the front door flew open. Adam was standing in the doorway. Soaking wet from head to toe and looking surly.

Naoto saw the truth immediately: Adam had been drinking. He did not usually drink but this was not the worst. Behind his bad mood was something more serious. Like a hint of madness. Suddenly Naoto was scared.

"Pack your bags," the Marine ordered. "We're taking off. I don't want to stay one minute longer in this country of lunatics!"

Adam came into the room. He staggered and grabbed the table to hold himself steady. Naoto had never seen him in such a state.

"Pack your bags, damn it! I'm bringing you with me right now!"

These words were so absurd that she could not even answer him. She never had the will or desire to leave

Okinawa. Moreover, they had never spoken a word about their future together.

Still holding onto the kitchen table Adam slowly shuffled toward her. "Hurry up, Naoto! Do what I tell you!"

His last sentence sounded threatening and Naoto really felt that she was in danger.

And then, all of a sudden, the Marine's arm started swinging through the air, sweeping over the table and knocking off the plates and glasses and his hand smashed into the sculpture that the young woman was working on.

"Stop, Adam! You're out of your mind! You've never hit me! Leave me alone!"

"I didn't hit you, Naoto. I just smashed one of your stupid sculptures like I'm going to smash all of them!"

"You're drunk, Adam! You're crazy! Get out of here! Leave me alone!"

Adam suddenly straightened up, apparently no longer in need of the table. Violently but methodically he started breaking Naoto's creations. One after another without missing a single one.

The young woman could do nothing but watch, powerless, helpless, at this fit of rage.

All her sculptures were destroyed and whatever had fallen down without breaking Adam stomped on furiously. The young Marine was going at the objects with such savage violence that Naoto panicked and ran to the front door.

Adam swung around and fast as lightning jumped at her, grabbing her blouse. His eyes were bloodshot.

"You want to run away, crazy thing? When I came over here to save your life!"

"You don't know what you're saying, Adam. You're drunk. You have to try to calm down."

Naoto was fully aware that it was not just alcohol that put Adam in this state. Even if he had plainly drunk way too much. Something must have happened. Something that she did not understand.

Adam stopped waving his arms but he kept hold of the girl. His eyes were wild and his face twitching.

Naoto suddenly broke down in tears. "You broke everything I care about. Why did you do that?"

With one hand still clutching her the young soldier turned his head slowly and looked at the room. In a quiet voice he said, "You ask me why?"

He had another fit of violence. But this time it was focused on her. He slapped her face as if she were the one being hysterical. Naoto, who could not escape, tried to protect herself as best she could. And then the hail of blows stopped.

"I'll tell you why," he said. He opened the front door and pushed her down the two flights of stairs.

Maybe if she got to the street she had a chance of escaping. A slight chance. She could also call for help. But when they stumbled onto the sidewalk, fear struggling with surprise, she was dragged inside the Marine's car without enough time to try anything.

At the wheel he did not seem to know what to do. He kissed her lightly on the forehead. Naoto was shocked. Adam had never raised his hand to her. And he had never rambled so confusedly to her.

"I'm sorry, Naoto. I wanted to save you despite yourself."

The young woman stayed silent. On and off her body was shaken by nervous spasms and hiccups had followed her tears.

"It's the apocalypse," he explained. "Look around you. Don't you see it's daytime? We have to get out of here. But first I had to destroy all your sculptures. I had to, understand."

Naoto did not understand. She looked around. In fact, a weird atmosphere had fallen over the neighborhood. Even if the word apocalypse was a little exaggerated, there was a buzz in the air. As if an attack had been committed close by. Through the car window she could see a small group of people in an animated discussion. Adam ended up starting the car and driving off into the streets where people were running around everywhere, clearly panicking. He drove like a madman, barely controlling his anxiety.

"Where are you taking me?" she managed to pronounce.

"To the base. So you'll understand. After that, we're going far, far away from here."

"But you know you can't just leave the army like that! And there's no reason for me to go with you. What's going on, Adam? You've become… You're acting really weird. You hit me!"

"I said I'm sorry. But you have to understand. Your sculptures… You can't make sculptures anymore."

"I don't get it. what's wrong with my sculptures? You said you liked them! You're talking nonsense! I want to get out of this car."

"No. We're going to the base, it's not far."

Naoto did not press him. The car cruised through the night, weaving through the pedestrians who were becoming more and more numerous, more and more excited. All the other drivers were as wild as Adam who clenched his teeth as the car lurched and reeled trying to avoid an accident.

They finally got to the base. Adam sped straight in and came to a screeching halt far beyond the area he was supposed to park.

There was no guard at the post, Naoto thought. *Anyone can coming waltzing in here* .

At the end of the Second World War, around 26 years earlier, the American base at Kyoda had been built on the ruins of an old submarine base abandoned by the Japanese during the war and left to rot. The American army had the opportunity to set up a base and house their men.

Naoto knew the base. She had come here many times to wait for Adam. She had never thought that it would be possible to get in so easily. Usually she had to wait patiently by the guard post. Tonight she felt like she was entering a museum open free to the public.

Adam got out, walked around the car and opened the door for her in a ludicrous display of chivalry, as if he were trying to make up for his violent, unacceptable behavior.

"Come on, Naoto. I'll show you. I have to get my stuff. In the meantime you can take a gander insider. It's no longer a military base. Now it's an art gallery. A real art gallery!"

The demented smile and wild eyes that deformed his appearance when he arrived at her place earlier were still etched on his face. When she saw him disappear inside a building she was sure that she would never see him again.

An army vehicle had just stopped less than ten yards away. What she did not know was that the man jumping out and slamming the door shut was none other than Smith Beffort.

Just like her the FBI agent had just been informed of the bizarre incidents taking place on the base. He had not even had time to visit the new "art gallery" yet. Because in Okinawa one event after another were occurring at breakneck speed and Beffort could not be everywhere at once.

Followed by other FBI agents Beffort had rushed to the old submarine base. A submarine base no longer. A military base that seemed to be under nobody's control. Tonight a wind of panic and confusion had blown through. And there were apparently no more regulations.

Naoto followed them and went inside the huge concrete building. She found herself in a big, vaulted corridor like the nave of a cathedral—at first from its appearance but then because of the weird feeling in the air.

People were gathered in this vast corridor, apparently lost in deep thought. When Naoto looked up at the ceiling her gaze was attracted by the astonishing statues and it was then that she understood why Adam had talked about her sculptures and destroyed them.

They were life-size statues of soldiers, embedded in concrete at different levels. Some of them were completely out of the wall, others only had a limb or head sticking out.

The young lady stood there petrified. What her eyes were seeing her brain refuse to admit. Because these statues were alive.

Naoto saw the suffering that deformed their faces, which looked like stone but whose slow agony was definitely of living beings. Arms and legs moved sluggishly.

There were at least 100 of them around her, forming a legion of the damned walled forever in the reinforced concrete. And there must have been more in all the other buildings on the Kyoda base.

What artist from hell could have created such monstrous works?

Naoto swore that she would sculpt again.

Chapter XI

Since arriving in Okinawa Smith Beffort had practically not slept. Over the hours that passed his brain was bombarded with an anarchic array of information and he had trouble analyzing it and making connections.

He was in a foul mood and his thoughts were as agitated as the storm brewing over Okinawa, which seemed never to go away.

"Is the weather always so crappy here?" he asked one of the representatives of the Okinawa Air Base who wanted to come with him to Kyoda.

"It's the first time the weather's so bad," the soldier answered. "We don't know where all these clouds and wind are coming from. It looks like they're having fun swirling around overhead."

Beffort felt the humidity soaking into his bones. Getting into the Jeep he realized that his clothes were wet. The lieutenant and the soldier were in the same condition.

"Bring me back to my hotel," Beffort said. "I'm dead tired, my clothes are soaked and I need to think for a while."

"Think about what, about everything that's happened?" the lieutenant asked after a long silence during which none of them had dared to say a word about what they had seen.

"I've seen too many things since I got here," Beffort said. "I don't really know what to think. And I need some rest to clear my head."

"What I meant was, do you think Madame Atomos is mixed up in all this?"

"It looks more like the devil's business but it's true that I've been confusing the two more and more lately. My colleague Yosho Akamatsu, who's checking out Hawaii, told me that the young man sent to the Kunako base was recruited by the Organization. So, there's no reason to doubt where this chaos comes from! And I have to interrogate that guy before they get to him. It wouldn't be the first time a suspect croaked in custody."

"We'll take you to Kunako tomorrow at the crack of dawn if the weather holds until then. The base is only accessible by boat or helicopter."

"I'd be grateful, lieutenant. We'll go out there tomorrow. Unless another disaster strikes in the meantime... But for now I'm going to lie down. I've got some sleep to catch up on."

When he was in his hotel room Beffort took a hot shower and called down to the front desk for them to take care of his clothes. After the bellhop came to get them he lay down on the bed.

Only seconds later he heard the rain come knocking, then hammering at the windowpanes. Oh well, he had seen worse in his life...

His thoughts were turning toward Mie, whom he had promised to call the next day. Then he hoped that the horrors he had seen over the last few hours would not disturb his sleep. His wish was granted: he dropped off right away into a deep, dreamless sleep.

A knock at the door woke him up sometime later. It was light out and his clock read 10 am. He jumped out of bed and threw on his bathrobe.

"What's going on?" he asked the bellhop in the corridor. "Is the General Staff asking for me?"

"They're waiting for you downstairs, Mr. Beffort. Two soldiers in the lobby."

"Very well. Ask them to wait. I'll be down in a jiffy."

Less than 15 minutes later Beffort went down and met the two Marines who drove him directly to Okinawa Air Base. It was there that the military had set up temporary headquarters to supervise the operations and coordinate the actions on the affected bases.

The FBI agent went straight to the mess and gulped down a big cup of bad coffee before going to the main office. General Merrill was there along with General Baxter whom Beffort knew well. Baxter had come to lend a hand to his colleagues who did not know which way to turn in the cataclysm they were facing.

Beffort noticed immediately that Baxter was the only one of the officers present who looked levelheaded. The general even had the presence of mind to give him a friendly smile and a firm handshake. Beffort was glad to see him here because he knew by experience that Baxter was going to be a valuable asset in this crisis.

"We can draw a few conclusions now," General Baxter told the dozen officers gathered around him, all as stiff as pawns on a chessboard. "The first thing I can tell you, and you must consider this a very serious aspect, is that the sun has come back."

General Baxter pointed to the big window that looked out on the huge city of Okinawa. Beffort realized that being so rudely dragged out of bed he had not taken account of the sudden change in weather. Indeed, the sky was blue again and the dark clouds of the day before had apparently vanished for good.

"For me it's a sign," the general went on. "The events started 72 hours ago now and they haven't let up since. At this moment what observations can we make about the series of attacks? Well, I'll say that of all the American bases in Okinawa five have been hit hard. Five of our bases are victims of unexplainable disasters and all the men there have disappeared over a certain period of time, only to reappear a few hours later in a horrifying state, but only on four of the bases. We are here, gentlemen, on the only base where the Marines who disappeared have still not given any sign of life. Now everything is calm. If I talk about the weather, if I point out the bright sun, it's because the baffling phenomenon occurred in Okinawa and the disturbance seems to have stopped. Things seem to be back to normal."

Baxter turned to Beffort, seeking his approval, but the agent stood unfazed, waiting for him to finish.

"Mr. Beffort here with us is in a position, thanks to his thorough knowledge of the Atomos Organization, to show us whether all these events were caused by her. In truth it'll only confirm our own suspicions."

The general took Beffort's arm and led him aside. He spoke in a low but firm voice.

"Mr. Beffort, very early this morning we went to the island of Kunako to estimate the damage. We found no survivors. It's likely that the young man we wanted to interrogate is dead also. However, we're still searching. I suggest you join the team of Marines who are leaving right now for the island."

Then aloud he addressed the officers again.

"I informed Mr. Beffort of our latest discovery. Let's hope it'll be the last. There are still a bunch of questions that remained unanswered but I trust the professionalism of our specialists and our soldiers who fight and sometimes give their lives in the service of…"

But Smith Beffort was not listening.

All his thoughts were focused on the Kunako base. The absence of survivors meant that the investigation would once again hit a dead-end.

Madame Atomos had succeeded in settling a score with the American forces implanted in Okinawa. Since the population of the island was calling for the US Army to leave, this came as no surprise. These bases were a perfect target for the Japanese woman. Once the military personnel in Okinawa were completely decimated, there was no explanation left. A job well done, basically, before moving on to other things.

But Beffort thought it a little strange that she had not claimed responsibility for any of the actions. Kanoto Yoshimuta was not a woman who let an opportunity to grandstand slip by. Beffort was sure that she would show up sooner or later.

"The other important point," Baxter continued, "that makes me think that it's all over is that there were five requests for exterminators from the outside. To my knowledge, no more. However, this is something we have to verify. In short, five workers were brought into five camps. Five workers brought in by Mr. Tan, well known to local police. And these men were equipped with an object, a device, I don't really know what, which couldn't be identified since they all disintegrated when we tried to study them. These devices, without a doubt, were the cause of the tragic events. As for the suicides by cyanide poisoning of four of the exterminators, they bring us straight back to Madame Atomos. It's a pity that we still haven't found the guy sent to Kunako who didn't kill himself."

"And what are we supposed to do now?" one of the officers asked.

"We've started to send the families back home to the US. The wives and children are not safe in Okinawa. We want to keep a minimum number of troops here, chosen from among the most competent personnel. It'll take us months to get the bases back in shape. That's our priority. Now, the FBI investigation has put us on a trail that leads to Hawaii. But that's not my job. To each his own."

"And you don't think we're running a risk by staying here?" a young lieutenant piped up. "If Madame Atomos decided to unleash the plagues of Egypt on us, or worse, wouldn't it be wiser to evacuate all our troops?"

"I find your question totally outrageous, lieutenant!" Baxter shouted. "The American government will never bow down to this woman! We will never abandon Okinawa! We soldiers will fight to the death to foil the plans of this diabolical woman and when all is said and done we will be victorious! Any other questions?"

"Yes. Does Mr. Beffort know if there's a chance that the Marines at the Okinawa Air Base will reappear?"

All eyes turned to the agent as if he could give them answers to all their questions.

"I don't know any more than you, gentlemen," Beffort responded. "I'm not privy to Madame Atomos' private thoughts. I don't know her intentions. It's been a long time since I've been tracking her and the harder I fight against her, the more I feel like she's slipping away from me. On every level. The FBI is working day and night to draw up a psychological profile. We now know the details of her past. I'm not working alone. We're a team, the Green Dragon, but there are also people in the bureau in Washington. And the farther we go retracing our enemy's career, the more I'm certain that we're missing a piece of the puzzle. Of course my deepest desire is to put an end to this heinous woman's activities, but I have to admit that in some way, when I find the missing piece, I'm scared of the truth awaiting me. Therefore, to answer your question, I'm an FBI agent, I do my job the best I can, but I can't tell you if the Marines will reappear some day."

The officers stood speechless, then slowly left the room. Baxter brought Beffort to the inner courtyard where a Jeep was waiting to take him to the port to join the team of soldiers heading for Kunako.

The island of Kunako appeared. It was less than one nautical mile away. Smith Beffort would have preferred to take a helicopter but none was available. All aircraft had been requisitioned to bring emergency aid to the affected bases.

The crossing had been very long but Beffort could now make out the outlines of Kunako. The speedboat was cruising at full throttle and cutting through the waves with all its power. The faces of the Marines on board were serious and pensive. All of them knew that they were about to face an unbearable sight, since the first troops helicoptered in had already made a frightening report about the extent of the disaster.

When the boat docked the men jumped off. Beffort was one of the first to set foot on the dock. A Jeep and some military trucks were there, waiting to bring the reinforcements to the base. Beffort let the soldiers gather around their chief. He climbed into the Jeep and ordered the driver to go straight to the base.

He heard the buzz of helicopters, unseen but near-by. Then a rescue copter jumped out in front of the Jeep like a giant insect.

The closer the Jeep got to the base, the more Beffort felt the turmoil. The first teams of soldiers that had arrived the day before were busy at work. The foul stench of rot invaded his nose and told of the horrible fate that some 500 Marines had met on the island.

Beffort had been warned by Baxter of the scale of the disaster. But the general did not know all the details of the abomination and all he said was that the men on the Kunako base were dead. This was only partially true.

Beffort had to be right next to the first corpse to understand the horror of what had happened. He saw, first, a few hundred yards away, two Marines leaning over the body of a soldier. Their movements were hectic and their faces terrified. When Beffort approached them, he saw with horror that the corpse was already eaten by worms. Hundreds of maggots covered the body and it looked like the man had been dead for days. But the two Marines fidgeting around him seemed, oddly enough, to be searching for some way to give him first aid.

It was then that Beffort understood.

In spite of all the atrocities that he had seen over the years, this vision filled him with dread. It would never go away.

Because the body lying on the ground was still alive.

Eaten away by worms crawling in its flesh, the soldier was still moving.

The agent did not have time to think. Other Marines were showing up, ready to lend a hand to their comrades and they were pushing and shoving him aside. Nevertheless, nothing these men did was of any use.

A few yards away Beffort spotted another group of soldiers leaning over another body. He ran to them and witnessed the same horrifying sight. This horror was repeating itself all over the camp.

Hundreds of corpses scattered over the ground, some already reduced to skeletons, others still alive, being devoured by vermin before the terrified eyes and the futile efforts of the rescue teams.

Orders were shouted in all directions. Marines tried to sort the living from the dead. But the task was not easy. Those still alive were barely moving but they made no sound, no moan, no groan, no death rattle, not even a whimper. Their vocal chords had been eaten as well.

And Beffort watched this awful, silent dance around the still moving corpses.

The sight was so frightening that everyone forgot about the stench that the island gave off. An island that once housed the best soldiers of the American army was now a giant graveyard under a bright sun where everyone standing had only one desire: to see their friends, their dying brothers finally breathe their last breath.

Beffort collapsed in the seat of an abandoned vehicle. A Jeep or something like that. He was not really sure of the make and model but he really did not give a damn. It felt like his brain was stuck in an ultimate defensive reaction.

I'm just a cop, after all, he thought. *There are things that my mind will refuse to admit. How could she commit such an abomination! How can anyone deal with such a horror!*

He sat for a moment, petrified by his distress. He gave himself a minute of rest and this was hardly a luxury if he wanted to get back in the fight under the best possible conditions.

He wondered whether Madame Atomos had anything human left in her or if she had gone over into the sphere of pure Evil? If this was the case, was it even worth fighting? Wasn't the confrontation unequal? Smith Beffort was just a cop and the diabolical Japanese woman had maybe gathered too much strength for him to challenge.

And then he looked at the young soldiers who were busy separating the living and the dead. Boys! As tormented as he was! But they were still fighting because there was nothing else to do.

True he was older and he had taken more blows than anyone should. But the FBI agent was fully aware that he just needed a breather and his desire to fight was not completely sapped. He was not done with the Japanese woman yet.

Beffort got out of the vehicle and marched toward the Marines.

The more hours passed, the more the Kunako base looked like a vast burying ground in the Tropics. The stench of rot mixed with the stifling heat forced the soldiers, in spite of the blazing sun and the thorough disgust they felt, to work even harder at their task.

Beffort felt the utmost anxiety. He wanted to find some immediate answers. He wanted to find a reason for this apocalypse. But the corpses piling up around him had nothing to say.

Everyone was running all over the place and the FBI agent had lost sight of the officers. Nevertheless, he forced himself into action. Some of the buildings had still not been examined but it was the same sight everywhere. Every opened door gave them the same shot of adrenaline, the same shiver down the spine.

Inside an office Beffort found a young Marine barely 20 years old lying on the ground. His semi-still body was teeming with worms from head to toe. He was still shaken by faint jerks as the vermin burrowed into his guts and ate his stomach. And yet the young man stared at Beffort with his blue eyes, begging, imploring, in a mute cry, to stop his unbearable suffering.

Without thinking twice Beffort drew his service revolver and fired.

It was as if he had given the signal. Right away, all over the base, shots rang out from the soldiers who were finally authorized to put an end to the dreadful torture of their unfortunate comrades.

The solution was certainly radical but faced with such an abomination no member of the rescue team could find anything better to do.

At headquarters in Okinawa General Merrill was contemplating the sky, glad to see that it had never been as clear since he arrived. The storm was gone for good and it seemed to have put an end to the terrible crisis afflicting the bases.

Now there were cats.

Wild cats had been seen on the other bases. No one really paid them any attention at first because there was an emergency to deal with. But today there might be time to think about these felines that were starting to fill up the bases that were supposed to house American soldiers, not serve as a shelter for abandoned animals.

This was also the opinion of Barger. Barger had been sent to Okinawa two days ago and he did not understand anything that was going on except that it was a lousy mess and his plans of getting back to Oregon before winter were still just a dream.

Private Barger's mission was to clean out the biggest buildings and inform his superiors of any suspicious discovery. For the moment there were only the damned cats that seemed to be getting more and more uppity. When Barger stepped into the corridor leading to the toilets a dozen of the tomcats ran past him, bumping into his legs as they went.

Barger had no intention of cleaning the toilettes. He just wanted to relieve himself and he did not look kindly on a cat or any other animal disturbing his peace during this intimate moment.

The felines, more and more or them, were crowded before the restroom door. There must have been at least 30 of them now. The soldier started kicking at them before opening the door but the cats were in no mood to let him by. When he finally entered the restroom, he found more of them, scampering off after spitting and screeching their discontent at the soldier.

Alone at last Barger was about to drop his pants when he caught sight of some tiny objects littering the floor, which might have been the reason why all the cats were so excited. Barger reached out to pick one up but his face suddenly twisted into a mask of horror.

A few minutes later General Baxter learned the news from Barger himself, although he had trouble speaking coherently and his whole body was trembling.

"General," Barger stammered, "the vanished soldiers are back on the base. Everything's… in order."

On pronouncing "order" Barger had a fit of hiccups. Then the hiccups turned into hysterical laughter. Before the general could question him he had already sunk into madness.

"Here! Come quick! There's one still alive!"

The shouts came from the kitchen. Beffort and some Marines near enough to hear rushed over to the heavy door to the cold room near the dining hall. By "alive" he meant a man who had not yet been afflicted and whose body showed no signs of change.

The young man in the cold room had apparently suffered nothing. He was definitely alive. But his body had dropped to a temperature well below zero. It was a miracle that he was still breathing and it would be another if he continued. Two nurses came running. The section commander bellowed for a doctor.

"We have to act fast," Beffort was watching the pale skin of the young man who had been placed on a stretcher. Then he turned to the commander, "We have to get this man to the main hospital in Okinawa urgently and contact the best doctors they've got. I don't know what his chances of survival are but I do know that right now this guy is our only hope of finding answers to what really happened in Kunako."

The young man with Asian features looked exactly like the description of Richard Tardif.

Chapter XII

The next day Beffort and Yosho made several phone calls back and forth. Moreover, police in Hawaii were in constant contact with Washington.

"I'm leaving Okinawa as soon as possible," Beffort told his Japanese colleague. "It's time to organize Richard Tardif's return to the US."

"You're certain now of the identity of the guy you found in the cold room?"

"Absolutely certain it's him. He's in stable condition. At least that's what the doctors at the Okinawa hospital say. In my opinion, the sooner he gets to Washington, the sooner we'll get out of this mess."

"It's up to you," Yosho responded. "Me too, I have two witnesses who need to be brought to Washington right away. Have you got a plan to guarantee their safe transport, Smith?"

"It'll be done within 24 hours. There are still a few details to iron out regarding security. You know as well as I do that witnesses who can help us usually don't have long to live. The Hawaii police received orders to give you all the help you need to transport them. Have you managed to get any information out of the two women?"

"I haven't interrogated the professor yet. She's in no condition for it. Like I told you, she got half her face bitten off by a rat and that doesn't really make it easy for her to talk. So, I'm waiting for the go-ahead from the doctor. I'm anxious to hear what she has to tell us. It'll certainly be interesting."

"Have you checked with the hospital about whether she can be moved?"

"It should be doable. With maximum precautions, of course."

"And your second witness… you said it was Richard Tardif's mother, right?"

"Exactly. She's a Japanese woman around 50 years old. She told us a few things but it's mostly superficial. If I understand her motivations, the guy you found half frozen is a kid she didn't want and she used him to serve the cause of the Atomos Organization. We also found Tardif's father but he seems completely outside everything."

"Do you know how deeply his mother is involved in the Organization?"

"If she's not jerking us around too much—but I don't think she is because we've been grilling her for 24 hours—her role is just to find meeting places for the Organization, landing strips in Hawaii, renting rooms and hangars, trucks and stuff like that… She deals with logistics, if you want. Apparently the Atomos gang has the habit of stopping over on the island to take care of business and so they need to collaborate with some local politicians and bigwigs. Furthermore, some of them have been disappearing lately or getting their brains blown out. The rats are abandoning ship."

"A lot of corruption in Hawaii, you think?"

"No more than anywhere else. Let's just say that the Organization has set up its network here. And that's also why I know they'll eliminate any inconvenient witnesses. In my opinion, if the guy's mother is still alive, it's because she doesn't have much to tell us."

"So, you're counting on the professor's statement?"

"Yes. At the hospital she's got 24/7 protection. That's why I'm asking you to work fast, Smith."

"Don't worry, I'll give you the details of the operation in few hours. When we see each other in Washington we'll try to get all the information out of these two women. Do you really think the Japanese woman doesn't have much to tell us?"

"There's one way to find out, Smith. Even more radical than truth serum. I'm letting her out into the parking lot to smoke a cigarette. After 15 minutes if she hasn't got her head blown off by Madame Atomos' killers, it because we have nothing more to learn from the poor girl."

"I still don't get the subtlety of your humor, Yosho!"

"But I'm not joking, Beffort. Not at all!"

During the day Mie got several phone calls from her husband. In the course of the last call he told her he was coming back to Washington the next day.

"I'm following the affair on the news," Mie said. "There's a newsflash every five minutes but no one seems to know or understand much. Are all these disasters connected to Madame Atomos?"

"Yes, no doubt about it, there's a connection," Smith responded. "But it's too complicated for me to explain over the phone. All I can tell you is that the situation is back to normal. Everything seems to be over. But the American army suffered heavy losses. More than 20,000 Marines are dead or disappeared around Okinawa."

"And the local population?"

"Completely untouched. Only certain military bases set up on the islands were affected by the... mysterious mutations. By an indescribable phenomenon that reached a new level of horror that I never imagined I'd see in my life. Can you believe that on the base in the middle of the city of Okinawa, when the Marines reappeared, they were only four inches tall? Soldiers the size of dolls and they got massacred by cats. All I can hope is that they were already dead when they were swallowed."

"When did they reappear? Why? They disappeared, right?"

"Yes. They disappeared from the base for 24 hours."

"And we can't suppose they were just hidden away somewhere?"

Beffort did not answer immediately. He had not considered this possibility.

"Are they all dead?" Mie asked.

"There's a sole survivor at the Okinawa Air Base. It was a massacre. They found nothing but mutilated, bloody bodies but the biggest one was no more than four inches tall."

"They were all different sizes."

"What? What do you mean?" Surprised, Beffort did not get where his wife was going.

"I mean that if the bodies are different sizes, some of them might be even tinier. Maybe some of them are less than an inch high and we still can't see them."

"That's possible. Anyway, the search goes on. But I doubt the Health Services of the Army or the Medical Corp of the Marines are giving priority to that kind of speculation. They've got a lot to do."

"But they're human beings, Smith!"

"I know, but there are decisions that are not mine to make. As an FBI agent my job now is to organize the transfer of the three witnesses back to DC. And believe me, it's not going to be easy."

In spite of this Beffort realized that his wife's hypothesis could be well founded and it at least deserved to be checked out.

He was also aware of the fact that he was exhausted, completely worn out, both his body and his nerves, and that it would not be easy for him to coordinate the police and the army working together. He would ask General Baxter for the soldiers to continue searching for possible survivors. Above all, he had to pursue Yosho's work and guarantee the witnesses' security.

It was 6:45 am. The sun had just peeked through the morning fog, which was slowly dissipating over the Big Island, when an ambulance parked right in front of the number 4 entrance to the Honolulu General Hospital.

A security team of eight police officers armed to the teeth was in charge of escorting the patient in room 217. A stretcher carried by two nurses was coming down the corridor at 6:52. At exactly 7:00 the stretcher was put into the ambulance waiting at the entrance. One of the policemen said a few words to the driver before sitting in the passenger seat while his colleagues stepped away. The vehicle had not started up yet.

Some FBI agents were standing with the uniformed officers, talking to other colleagues through walkie-talkies. A few quick hand signs and as a wind started to blow through the parking lot, it seemed like everyone scattered. The ambulance was alone, totally abandoned.

But three FBI men were already in the back, ready to take the patient to the airport. The ambulance, therefore, had a driver and four cops, which was not too many to cover the 26 miles separating them from the small Kuliouou airport.

The FBI had decided not to take Anna to the main Honolulu airport where a commando strike by the Atomos Organization was always to be feared. By changing their modus operandi at the last minute the chances of attack were reduced considerably. The trip on the highway was the most critical part of the operation now but the FBI was counting on the fact that the Atomos gang would be caught off guard by the abrupt and tactful change of plans. In fact, very few people knew about the last minute transfer that should take less than an hour to accomplish.

Vernon Dyer was the youngest cop who had sat inside the ambulance. He had just come out of the police academy in Pittsburg and was an FBI inspector in training for less than a year. During the few months that he had been stationed in Honolulu he had accomplished all kinds of physical exploits that he would never have believed he was capable of. Vernon was an athlete and also a daredevil whose energy the FBI knew perfectly well how to channel. He was highly motivated and ready for all kinds of sacrifices.

However, he was levelheaded enough to understand that an operation like this one was bound to fail. If the Atomos Organization wanted to silence a witness, his hide along with all his colleagues was not worth a plug nickel. Vernon knew the reputation of the Atomos gang and no squadron of cops or soldiers was going to stop it.

The ambulance had been cruising now for a full half hour on the straight Kalanianaole Highway. It was being followed by an unmarked car that kept a safe distance of around 150 feet. If they had added three tanks and two helicopters, it would have changed nothing. At least this is what Vernon Dyer was thinking at the moment the attack broke out.

Sitting next to the driver he watched him out of the corner of his eye. The guy was no older than him. And he was not even a cop, just an ambulance driver. Vernon thought that to accept such a mission when he did not have to the poor fellow must be suicidal or a total blockhead. This was not how Vernon saw his job. He had no problem risking his life. The only thing was that if there had to be lives lost, he at least wanted it to serve a good purpose.

The two vehicles were not driving more than 30 miles an hour. They could not go faster because of the bad roads and for the health of the patient that compelled them to avoid potholes.

They were about halfway there when Vernon Dyer felt a sudden panic attack. His hands started to tremble and he had to take a leak badly. First he turned to the driver, then to his colleagues in the back.

"I need to piss," he said. "Tell the guys in the car that we're taking five. I can't hold it."

One of his colleagues sitting next to the wounded girl gave him a cold smile. Then he shot out his hand and grabbed the lapels of his jacket.

"Listen, jerk, we're all in the same boat here. The mission is almost over, so you can piss in your pants and not put us in any danger!"

To everyone's surprise Vernon shook him off and started yelling at him.

"What's the point of all of us getting killed, you bunch of fools! I'm 21 years old, I want to live, I don't want to die for bullshit! And I have to piss! So call the car behind us and tell them we're pulling over!"

The other agent was already on the walkie-talkie warning the other car. "Hey guys, we've got a little problem here. There's a kid who needs to take a whiz and he's losing it. We're asking for authorization for a short break."

"Don't stop for anything!" the other spit out. "The kid can hold it until we get to the airport. And if he's losing control, you control him! I repeat, don't stop no matter what!"

But Vernon has started to climb over the seat to jump in the back. He was swinging his fists in the air and his colleagues were just glad that he had not attacked the driver who had to keep the ambulance on the road.

They tried to hold the young man down. "Calm down, okay!" one of them yelled, trying to pin his arms.

"What are you doing up there?" a voice came over the speaker. "We can't see what's happening in the ambulance."

"I think it's okay. We've got a hold of the kid but he's not really calmed down yet. We don't know what happened. It came over him all of a sudden, a panic attack or his nerves cracked. But it's all right now, the situation is under control."

"Listen you guys, you're coming up on the first turns at Laukahi Park. If something's going to happen, I'll bet it'll be on this stretch of road. So try to hold out for the next few miles. After that I think we'll be out of the woods."

Vernon was still pinned to the ground by his colleagues, and still kicking up a storm.

"How's it going up there?" one of them asked the driver. "Can you drive okay with all this ruckus?"

"I'll manage."

Vernon ended up settling down. There was a lapse of time when they thought his fit was over. Then the strong stench of urine spread through the ambulance. All they could hear was the sound of the engine humming along. But Vernon's left leg suddenly shot out and kicked the back of the driver's head. By reflex he jerked the steering wheel hard and the vehicle swerved off toward the embankment as the FBI men in the car behind watched on helplessly.

"Shit! This time they've had it!" one of the shouted. "The ambulance is going to flip over!"

The ambulance driver was not an expert. He did manage, however, to straighten it out in a way that owed more to luck than any real skill. The startled FBI agents saw the ambulance ease its way back into the lane after defying the laws of gravity and of highway safety. They tried to get in contact with it but there was nothing but silence for a few minutes.

After a few more miles they finally arrived at the airport. All the men felt a little relieved. Their mission was coming to an end and soon they could go home.

The Honolulu Central Police Station was still dark. In one of the few lighted rooms Yosho Akamatsu was chain smoking cigarettes. He had to handle the transfer of the two women under conditions deemed dangerous. Smith Beffort had given him instructions but everything had happened a little too fast for him.

But there was no other way to do it. Yosho took another drag on his smoke. These women had to be in Washington by tomorrow evening. Once there they would be placed under maximum security.

He had got authorization from the doctors to talk briefly with the young professor. Just a few questions for her. She seemed sincere and quite lost, with no prospects but a ruined career and a dark future. She obviously did not tell him everything but in his opinion she was the more interesting of the two witnesses insofar as she was the one who could put him on the trail of Madame Atomos.

The other woman talked a lot. Without a doubt she was a good real estate agent but she did not seem to know much outside of the few missions the Organization had put her on. From what Yosho could gather, her life had not been easy so she went over to the other side, not even hesitating to sacrifice her son. A pretty ugly family history that did not concern the Japanese policeman but neither did it exonerate this woman of all the things she had done. She was over and done with and did not have anything interesting to tell him. There were just a few details he wanted to set straight with her.

Yosho headed toward the office where his partner had been interrogating the Japanese woman for an hour. She was being heard for the umpteenth time and each time her eyes were empty, eyes of someone who knew that they had nothing to lose and it was all over.

To his great surprise the office was deserted. Yosho heard a typewriter clacking in the backroom and he called in the police officer who was typing an overdue report on his Underwood.

"Have you seen Sergeant Murphy and the suspect?"

"They went out to smoke, I think."

"To smoke? Where?"

"Outside, I think."

"You think! Are you pulling my leg? I'm talking about Sergeant Murphy and a woman who's a suspected criminal but especially a witness who has to be protected! What are they doing going outside to smoke?"

The policeman looked a little offended. "The first of the year there was a new memo forbidding us to smoke in the building. Of course for you they bend the rules since you're from the Japanese police. But I think it's wrong and you should do like everyone else."

Yosho was not listening. He was already rushing down the empty corridors of the headquarters. His hurried footsteps echoed through the space, slipped on the tiles, almost tripping a few times before catching his balance at the last second.

Damn, where was the exit? And where did the stupid sergeant go to smoke a cigarette with a suspect? He had told him in no uncertain terms that such behavior was forbidden, especially with a state's witness against the Atomos Organization.

He called Murphy's name through the desolate corridors. In vain. Yosho found a metal door that opened onto an exterior platform where he could see the sky still dotted with stars.

Yosho was now in the open air, on a narrow walkway between the fifth and sixth floors. He instinctively looked down and his gaze stopped on a small inner courtyard behind the building. It was only two floors below him. A few people were starting to gather in it. At this early hour there were not many, of course. Maybe two or three policemen and a cleaning woman.

As for the lifeless body that they were looking at, lying in the middle of the courtyard, it was indeed the mother of Richard Tardif. The woman whom Richard had mistaken for Madame Atomos when she wanted to see her son one last time in Anna's house—she had fallen victim to the Organization. Given her position, she had been a perfect target for one of Madame Atomos' hired killers. Moreover, there was a very good chance that the assassin was still in the area. Maybe even on the walkway where Yosho was standing at the moment.

In the panic breaking out in the back of the ambulance before arriving at the airport, Vernon Dyer was knocked out cold by his colleagues. Now he was in a deep sleep.

The vehicle slowed down to a stop on the tarmac and the unmarked car escorting it parked nearby. The men climbed calmly out of the vehicles and the FBI agents went up to Vernon who was gradually regaining consciousness.

"Got to take the stretcher to those buildings," one of the federal agents ordered. "We'll follow you. Something still might happen."

With calm and precise movements the policemen brought out the stretcher, adjusted the wheels and started toward the offices.

"If they were going to do something, they would've already done it," the agent apparently in charge said. "I think it's too late now."

"Let's wait and see," his colleague responded as he lit a cigarette. "As long as the stretcher isn't in the plane, nothing is certain."

"I don't know. I have the feeling that nothing's going to happen."

The stretcher had reached the main building that they had to go around in order to head straight for the airplane waiting for them 100 yards away. Vernon was back to himself. Nobody came to ask him anything. Nobody gave it a thought. But he realized that his cowardice and his fear could have fouled up the mission.

He rubbed his sore jaw. He was KO'd by his colleagues and he pissed his pants! He figured that he could forget all about a promotion. Oddly, he did not think it was a big deal. The most important thing for him was that he was still alive. For the rest, he would go back to Pittsburg and move back in with his parents.

He watched the group which was no more than ten yards from the stairs. Vernon knew that nothing happened but he was not fooling himself. He was still alive but he knew that the mission was, in a way, a failure.

He caught up to his colleagues as the stretcher was slid into the airplane. "This time we made it!" he told the FBI agents waiting on the tarmac. "Sorry for almost botching the mission."

"Nah, it wouldn't have made much of a difference," the chief replied, unfazed. "Apparently they didn't take the bait. You can go home and get a good night's sleep. In fact, we could all use a good night's sleep tonight."

"Yeah, they didn't bite. I wouldn't like to be in the Japanese cop's shoes right now. He won't be getting any sleep. Unless he's lying in a coffin…"

A few miles away Yosho was driving peacefully, without any escort, in a beige Chevy Camaro. Nothing in his behavior would lead one to believe that he was very nervous. He even wanted to give himself a little treat: to put a cassette in the car stereo.

"Do you like the Ramones?" he asked his passenger. "It's a new band from New York. They still haven't made a record. It's just a pirated cassette from one of their shows at CBGB last winter."

He got no answer but continued.

"You know, I don't know any more about them than you. It's just that I read some notes on the case that I found in the glove box. I'm not a fan but it's something to talk about, to lighten the mood."

In the back seat Anna was still trembling. She was pumped full of pills so she was not feeling any pain. Big black sunglasses covered the bandages over her face wounds. She was fully aware that her life would be lived in total darkness from now on. She would also have to get used to being careful of all the sounds coming from outside.

Yosho pushed in the cassette.

At the moment he still did not know if the Atomos Organization would get caught in the trap set by the FBI. The survival of the witness was solely his responsibility and rested entirely on his shoulders.

When the first chords of "Chine Rocks" boomed through the car, Yosho could even smile a little. But the day was far from over.

Chapter XIII

When Richard's mother was killed in Honolulu early in the morning, Yosho Akamatsu had called Beffort right away and they decided on an emergency transfer. The FBI agent did not want to take any risks. The Organization was on the alert and it was ready to make all the witnesses disappear. The murder of the Japanese woman proved that Beffort was right.

He also knew that if Madame Atomos had decided to go into action, no armor and no police force, as strong as they might be, would be able to stop her. They needed to be sneaky. Make the Organization believe that the witness was in an ambulance headed toward one of the airports at any given time to be shipped off by plane.

The same problem happened to befall a guy in Okinawa: he was in critical condition and he might just hold the key to the mystery. This man needed serious medical assistance during the trip.

Beffort saw an opportunity. An American submarine, the USS Los Angeles, was cruising off the coast of Okinawa and could take over the transport of the half-frozen body of Richard Tardif, in complete secrecy of course. In less than 24 hours the submarine could reach Hawaii and pick up Anna while the Organization was searching for her in the skies, on one of the flights heading toward the mainland.

It was a good plan. Not 100% sure of course, but in a pinch it was the only one that made sense.

Therefore, Yosho had to drive Anna to the spot where she would be picked up by the submarine. For this he was using a car that the Honolulu police had given him while an ambulance, as a precaution, got on the road as a decoy.

For the rest they just had to cross their fingers and leave it up to higher powers... along with the professionalism of the FBI agents.

It was now more than 12 hours since Beffort got on board the submarine. The first phase of the operation went smoothly. Richard had been boarded in a big cooling box that looked strangely like an Egyptian sarcophagus, by forgetting of course about all the instruments and valves that kept the inside the right temperature.

The plan had been drawn up at the last minute. Most of the sailors on the submarine had been given leave and stayed on the dock, replaced by specialists, doctors and officers on board the USS Los Angeles.

Beffort constantly asked the medical personnel about the state of the patient. The doctors had opted for a solution that left Richard in a box where the temperature was close to zero. This treatment sounded like science fiction and was bizarre but it fit perfectly with what was expected whenever Madame Atomos was involved.

The specialists had finally figured out the spooky method used on the soldiers of Kunaki that had killed them all.

"You see, Mr. Beffort," Dr. Ozi had explained, "normally, after death, the tissues in the body break down. It starts right away, around four minutes after death. As the oxygen-deprived cells die, bacteria and other microorganisms attack the tissues. It's the start of decomposition. You know the process. The face swells, the tongue sticks out, blisters form under the skin, the body turns black. In brief, all very normal. Well, in the case we're facing today, it seems that the bacteria that eat the tissue got the signal that the individual had died and they could start feasting. So, they attacked on the inside, very quickly, while the poor men were still alive."

"It's incredible!" Beffort exclaimed.

"Incredible and terrible for these poor guys who could feel their guts being devoured by bacteria. Then the flies went at them like they do on real corpses and laid their eggs in the orifices, eyes or wounds. The larvae hatched in record time. I'll spare you the details since you were there like myself on the island. What saved this young man was the smart idea he got to lock himself in a cold room. It stopped the process. The cold put the bacteria to sleep."

"But they're only asleep!"

"That's right, Mr. Beffort. Bringing this guy back to normal temperature would wake up all the microorganisms and decomposition would be off and running. It's already begun and when you ask about interrogating him, well, I doubt you'll get much information out of him. Even though his brain is still functioning normally, there's a good chance that it's been affected by the phenomenon."

"So, when can we interrogate him?"

"I've already given the go ahead for the transfer, Mr. Beffort. He can be taken back to the US in the cold box we put him in. But I'll need you to wait a little longer to question him. It's not so simple. This young man has to be kept at a high enough temperature not to kill him but low enough to prevent the bacteria from waking up."

Beffort had to give in. He understood the situation. The game was not over and this guy could croak at any moment. Before even one question could be asked. He also understood that if his brain were altered, no clear answers could be expected.

Then he got the phone the call from Yosho telling him about the death of the first witness and he got the brilliant idea to board everyone on the submarine. Now the die was cast. The submarine was less than five miles off the coast of Hawaii and if things continued to go well, in less than an hour the FBI agent would be joining him Japanese colleague.

The Mercury was heading to the meeting point. Yosho had plenty of gas and was driving through the traffic like an ordinary tourist. In the evening he came in view of the beach they had selected. Traffic had become lighter, not because of the late hour but because the area was not particularly touristic.

Yosho parked the Mercury in the lot. They had more than 100 yards to walk. Despite her blindness Anna was able to move normally. And Yosho was there to act as her guide.

He had spoken little to the young lady during the trip and he was surprised to hear her groan when she got out of the car. When he whispered to her that everything was going to be okay, he surprised himself by his compassionate tone, as if he was still in the hospital at the bedside of a seriously sick woman.

Huge waves broke on the beach with a furious roar. The submarine was certainly in the area already but the rough seas were allowing no boat to land.

Yosho knew by heart his instructions. When he heard the humming of the helicopter that was supposed to bring them on board, he did not take his eye off the surrounding area.

Beffort was waiting for him too. The USS Los Angeles, the nuclear attack submarine that had been assigned to their mission, had surfaced more than one nautical mile off the coast. Out here the sea was calmer, the submarine stable and in a few minutes the crew would be able to proceed with the operation.

The helicopter came out of the darkening sky. It was a small one and its engine made no more noise than a big hornet. It hovered for a good half hour over the submarine, enough time to lower down Yosho and his ward.

The operation went off without a hitch and the young lady was immediately taken care of by two nurses who brought her down inside the ship while Yosho went to find Beffort waiting for him on the bridge.

"I'm glad to see you again, Yosho. Everything seems to be going as planned for the moment."

"Sure but it doesn't make me feel any better about what happened in Okinawa. We lost a witness in Hawaii and these two here might not be of much use to us."

"Okay but it's all we've got. A guy half-frozen and a blind girl who's not too clued in. It's a pretty weird situation and it's forced us to transform this submarine into a floating hospital. The good thing is that Madame Atomos hasn't shown up to silence them... so far."

"Maybe she doesn't think she has to. You know, the branch of the Organization set up in Hawaii is completely broken up. Tardif's mother got taken out in Honolulu, right in the police station, and I'm afraid that our final two witnesses don't have anything to tell us."

"You're just guessing, Yosho. At least now they're safe."

"And where are we bringing them in this submarine?"

"I've given it a lot of thought and with the military authorities we agreed that the best solution would be take them to one of our bases in Alaska in a day or two. In the meantime we're all set up on board to protect them. We have the necessary material and qualified personnel. I think it's the best place right now to keep them safe and carry out our mission."

Smith Beffort led his colleague to his quarters. The two men were staying with the rest of the crew, meaning in tiny cabins. But they were experienced and this was not the first time that they would have to make do with Spartan comforts.

The submarine had undergone a few quick changes to be transformed into a medical ship for the trip. But the USS Los Angeles kept its battle potential.

Anna and Richard had nice quarters adapted to their state of health. They were put in separate cabins located at the back of the boat. The spaces had to be modified for the patients to feel relatively comfortable. They had transformed the air regeneration system, the complex apparatus that allowed the sub to stay submerged for months at a time. In the context of this mission there was no reason to keep it, so they had removed it to give a little more space. Of course this did not prevent the submarine from being able to dive in deep water in case of a problem and the adjustments did not reduce its defensive capacities.

The medical staff was composed of five nurses and three doctors who were studying the extraordinary mutation that had affected Richard, which forced them to keep the kid alive and make sure that any police interrogations did not endanger his fragile balance.

Inside the cold box Richard stayed in moderate hypothermia. He was conscious and the doctors came now and again to say a few words to him, making sure that the young man was keeping a grasp on reality.

The box, which the doctors called a sarcophagus among themselves, was kept at a constant temperature that could be regulated according to the subject's reactions. Richard's molecular activity was reduced but this physical condition suggested that the rotting process was already well underway. The green blemish on his belly left no doubt about it. Small blisters had formed in different places under his skin and the flesh was starting to peel off. However, in the middle of his greenish, swollen face his eyes remained vivid—only his sight was spared by the devastating process.

"Can you hear me, Richard?" one of the doctors asked standing next to him.

The young man was awake, gazing at Dr. Ozi.

"We're bringing you back to the United States. The trip will take a few days. We were able to stop the necrosis that's destroying your cells. I won't go into details because you won't understand but under no circumstances should you move. It would be absolutely lethal to you. Do you understand, Richard?"

The young man gave no particular sign. Just a vague flutter of his eyelids. But the message seemed to have got through. Dr. Ozi went over to his colleague who was sitting in the back of the cabin.

"Just to be sure we'll give him another shot of morphine. Even if the process is slowed down, half his organs have been affected. It's a miracle this box is keeping him alive and I'm not at all sure about his chances of surviving the trip."

"Maybe we could authorize the cops to interrogate him while there's still time," the other doctor suggested.

"Maybe. The truth is I don't know what to do," Dr. Ozi responded. "The kid is strong but he needs rest. An interrogation might prove fatal. Let's wait a few hours before making a decision. Anyway, they've got the girl. In spite of her condition she's much more normal, so to speak."

In the same corridor, less than 10 yards away, was Anna's cabin. The trip with the Japanese agent who was responsible for protecting her had gone pretty well but the latest development had been strenuous and she was trying to deal with it bravely.

She was lying down again with the bandages taken off her eyes now but still she was plunged in darkness.

The ophthalmologist at her side was examining her face, whose upper part had been gashed by the rat teeth. He could call it nothing else but irreversible damage. The eyeballs, laid bare, were no longer protected by eyelids and the orbits were swollen. There were also several lesions under the left eye, the cheek needing an emergency operation. Before suffering another interrogation this young lady had to undergo surgery.

The painkillers were doing their job. Anna was resting, her head on the pillow, her mind in the grips of a weird reverie. Was this situation she was in all part of a nightmare?

In the tight quarters that they shared Beffort and Yosho were glad to be able to complete their mission side by side. So far they had only exchanged a few phone calls, mostly to plan their common strategy.

Beffort was able to explain to his colleague in detail everything that he figured implicated Madame Atomos in the apocalypse that had struck Okinawa.

"Even the weather was disturbed during the last few days. The sky was black, constantly filled with huge clouds. Lightening and strong winds. As if the diabolical woman had found a way to cripple the atmosphere."

"But the weather conditions are not really the heart of the problem…"

"That's for sure. The most horrible thing was the number of casualties and the changes they went through. There has to be a reason for all this. The FBI investigation is our number one priority right now. There are several teams already in place in Okinawa."

Then Beffort described more precisely the unbelievable transformations of the bodies of the American soldiers.

"But the weirdest thing," he said, "was what was seen on the Bhuto base. I wonder if at this stage we can still talk about physiological mutations. It's probably more accurate to call them 'ghosts' or 'spirits' but I don't believe in that kind of thing. Still, the 'spirits' in question—if we accept this is what they were—had been separated from the soldiers' bodies."

"In fact," the Japanese agent replied, "at this stage and since we have no choice, let's call them ghosts. But do these ghosts really have anything to do with Madame Atomos?"

"You know, Yosho, around two years ago I witnessed some really strange phenomena in Nevada, in the town of Salvation, while I was chasing the abominable Japanese woman. Until then I had always been—and I wasn't the only one—astonished by our enemy's power. But it was mainly about advanced technology. Science beyond anything we could imagine. But still science. Now, since what happened in Salvation I have the feeling that Madame Atomos is working on a different level.

In that deserted town there were dark forces. Unexplainable phenomena."

"You're using words that I never thought I'd hear come out of your mouth, Smith. Dark forces? It's against that kind of superstitious reaction that we're always fighting. Against manipulations of weak minds. I can listen to you talk about technology that defies our feeble knowledge, but dark forces? I think you're reaching."

The FBI agent sat silent for a moment. Then he smiled at his colleague, "You're right, Yosho. It would be the end for us if Madame Atomos made a pact with the forces of Evil!"

"I think you're joking now, Smith. Remember that everything has a rational explanation and we'll find it eventually."

"Sure, sure," Beffort replied.

The memory of the Salvation sheriff came rushing back. He and his wife must now be buried under several feet of earth. And with them all the Indian legends that the tribe from which Ralph Bender came had handed down from one generation to the next.

Smith said nothing for a while and when he spoke it was only small talk, which made Yosho suddenly feel uncomfortable.

The commanding officer of the USS Los Angeles was fixing a few internal problems with the doctors and the police.

The submarine, despite the changes that these civilians had made, was still under strict discipline for all duties regarding the crew. The captain, therefore, asked the doctors and the police not to leave their quarters during the 24-hour period needed for the necessary maneuvers.

Smith Beffort, Yosho Akamatsu and the all the medical personnel willingly agreed. All the more so since everyone needed a rest after the last few hours.

And the USS Los Angeles sailed on toward Alaska.

Chapter XIV

Richard was stuck in a no man's land between being awake and being out cold. At least that was what he told himself. It was hard to know what had really happened over the past few days, what was real and what was not.

He had vague memories of the Kunako base, of being put into the cold box. And then, oddly enough, the dream came back. A dream that he knew well and that become more and more real as time ticked away. It was a very nice dream that brought back the only happy memory he had of his parents. It was a long time ago in California. The three of them had gone for a walk on the coast. His father, his mother and he, all three together, maybe for the only time in their life at this moment of shared happiness.

But maybe none of it happened? Maybe the dream was really a lie? But Richard had hung on to it for years.

The sun was shining on the landscape. An intense heat; a deserted, idyllic beach; somewhere in California. His mother, as beautiful as ever, and his father, his face finally relaxed. And in this magic moment Richard just wanted to stand there and watch them.

Since he was put into the cold box this dream not only would not leave him but it became more and more real. The summer heat offset the intense cold of the fridge.

Even if he did not understand every detail, the young man knew that he was in a critical situation. If he had to die, it may as well be like this. He knew that his body was no longer completely his. He had overheard the doctors talking and he understood. But the more time passed, the more this place, this box fitted with all this sophisticated equipment to keep him alive, everything seemed to be fading away slowly into the California beach that was becoming his sole reality.

Without a doubt it was the effect of the morphine or some other drug that the doctors had given him.

Richard was trying to talk to his parents. Both of them were standing on the beach and laughing heartily. The young man knew that it was all a dream because no sound came out of their mouths.

"There's no noise. And there's nobody on this damn beach," he told himself. "But I still have to go and talk to them, to tell them that I'm here."

And then he noticed something weird. Dreams are always weird! His parents had both their feet stuck in the sand up to the ankles. And they kept laughing like it was nothing. When he got a little closer his mother finally saw him. Still laughing, she pointed to something behind him. Richard turned to look.

A lounge chair was facing the sea. Someone was on the beach next to them, lying in the chair. But from where he was he could not see who it was.

When Richard turned back to his parents they were buried a little deeper in the sand, which reached up to their knees now. Richard understood what was happening with this quicksand. He wanted to warn his parents but no sound came out of his mouth. It was also impossible for him to get any closer and they did not seem to realize the danger they were in. They just laughed and laughed.

His mother suddenly said something to him, pointing again at the chair where the unidentified person was still lying down. Her voice was distorted. Like a tape slowed down. But it was normal because this was a dream! And yet, he clearly understood what she was saying.

"Go get her, Richard. Go get her. There's not much time left."

He could still not make out who was in the chair. It was a woman, no doubt, from what his mother said and from the long, smooth, tan legs that he could see.

"Go get her, Richard. You don't have much time," his mother repeated tirelessly.

The young man looked at his feet. They, too, were buried in the sand. As for his parents, their legs had now completely disappeared. But they both kept laughing.

And it was then that Richard became fully aware of what was happening.

Anna had finally managed to relax. She did not feel any pain in her body. Just darkness. A darkness that would be her universe for the rest of her life.

She was fully aware of the condition of her eyes and of her own responsibility for what had happened. She had chosen her path. A militant path that she had very quickly regretted having taken because it did not really fit with her aspirations.

And they took advantage of it. The members of the Organization took over.

Anna wanted to give a lesson to the United States of America, which did not always act in an honest way. She wanted to show her opposition.

And today she was blind, with half her face ripped off.

The cops had come to interrogate her and now she was going to end up safe in a federal prison. A hell of an experience! But anyway, what future was there for a blind girl?

She was not even sure that she fully realized the extent of the damage. She had been a professor, she was disfigured by a rat and it was hard for her to imagine spending the rest of her life in the dark.

She lay down on the cot, almost peaceful but there was something inside her that would not give up hope. She had been transported in the air, hanging by a rope. In a few minutes she went from a helicopter into a military submarine. She could still feel the wind striking her face while she heard the noise of waves somewhere in the distance.

This was the first time that her life had taken such a dramatic turn. She could die at any moment and she did not care at all.

All of a sudden she wondered if she would face the death penalty. Then she realized that this was a completely ridiculous thought.

For a long time the pain had left her alone. The nurse on duty had left the cabin and she remained in total silence. They say the blind develop other senses that, in particular, can warn them of danger. Anna's mind was wandering from one idea to another when she had a strange feeling. It was not really a presence. More like a vibration coming closer, still far away but headed for her cabin.

Damn, she had never before felt so jittery! It must be due to her recent blindness. She was feeling completely terrified. She thought she was going to scream. She should do it fast, even if it meant alarming the entire crew. Because the thing she felt coming seemed to be moving fast and this thing wanted to hurt her.

Richard wanted so badly to obey his mother. He moved to the lounge chair but his legs were too deep in the sand now for him to go as quickly as he wanted.

Logically he should have felt sorry for his parents. His father was about to drown in the sand and his mother, already buried up to her neck, would soon join him. But Richard did not really feel sad because he knew that there was no other way.

His beautiful, smiling mother kept staring at him, saying the same thing, "Go get her, Richard. Bring her with you. You don't have much time."

Richard knew that he was continuing to watch his mother being entirely covered in sand. His father was already in another dimension and the young man felt no grief. He just felt a little pang of emotion when his mother's pretty face disappeared from sight. But he would always remember her eyes full of love.

Anyway, it would not be long before he joined his parents. There was only one small thing he had to do.

He recognized Anna in the lounge chair. She was sleeping, exhausted by the heat. Her skin, although already tan, was marked with nasty red stripes from the intensity of the sunrays.

"It's certainly better to disappear in the sand," he told himself. "When the sun is so hot, you're better off hiding in the depths of the earth."

However, he had to go to her and bring her into the shade. It was not good to stay lying in the sun like this. Anna was going to burn her skin.

And then he had something to prove to her. He had to show her that he could help her. He would carry her into the depths to keep her safe.

In spite of the sand grabbing his feet and hobbling his step, Richard was moving again. He was only a few yards away from her and he was confident.

Her hands were shaky and she had trouble controlling her movements. Her fingers were feeling along the safety bars on the sides of her bed and trying desperately to get a grip. It was no longer her sixth sense of a blind girl that was warning her. Anna felt a presence in the room and she knew what it was. In fact, even if she did not understand much of what was happening around her, she had felt it from the start.

She called Richard's name a few times, even shouted. Someone had to hear her. A nurse or a sailor would come rushing into the room to help her. Because it was help that she needed.

But it was a corpse that entered the room. She could feel it. Just the ghastly odor that stank up the air when the door opened. The odor of vermin and decay.

Anna sat up straight in bed and brought one hand up to her face because her eyes were starting to hurt again. Her emotion and fear seemed to have awakened the pain.

All of sudden she felt a hand grab her arm. She started screaming, jumped out of bed and tried to run away without paying any attention to the obstacles scattered around the cabin, which she could not see in her darkness.

She flattened herself against a wall that felt like a mere partition. Her whole body was trembling with horror and disgust. She had the feeling that the hand that had clutched her had left tiny living creatures on her wrist. She screamed louder and waved her arms in front of her.

Richard was there. She was sure of it. She smelled his rotting body. She did not know why but she was certain that it had to be him. And she had the horrible impression of already being in a tomb.

It was Smith Beffort who first heard the screams.

The two agents came running out of their cabin and headed straight for the source of the cries. The crew, nurses and doctors reacted immediately and the narrow corridor was quickly overcrowded. Beffort and Yosho banged on the door.

"It's locked on the inside!" Yosho yelled. "How can we open this door?"

"They're electronic locks," a sailor who had made it to the cabin answered. "A badge won't do it. We've got to cut the electricity in this part of the sub."

The sailor was struggling to open or unblock the locking mechanism when one of the doctors came up to the agents. He whispered to Beffort, "The young man got out of the box. It's suicide. He's only got half an hour before he's completely rotted away."

The FBI agent thought of the living corpses he had seen with horror on the island of Kunako. Inside the cabin Anna was still screaming, intermittently, while the awful stench of carrion was starting to fill the corridor.

"Try to get out," Yosho yelled. "What the hell's up with the electricity? Can't anyone on board open this damn door? Anna, come on, open the door for us!"

"It's no good getting upset," Beffort said. "She can't see anything and the place is unfamiliar. It'd be a miracle if she even made it to the door."

The screams behind the door became agonizing. The men felt a grisly shiver run down their spines.

His body was now entirely buried in the sand except for his head and shoulders. Richard held his arms in the air to keep them functional as long as possible. And he had managed to reach the chair.

Anna was smiling at him but her face was still empty of emotion. Maybe because of her two hollow eye sockets.

The young man held out his hand and when it got near hers he grabbed her wrist hard. Anna was still not moving but fear was now clearly seen on her face. The scene was starting to darken on all sides.

"You have to follow me," Richard asserted. "I've done everything I could for you. My parents are already gone. We have to join them. You have no choice, Anna."

The beach was shaken with strange vibrations and Richard knew that they would not be safe for long if they did not hurry up. Everything was changing and the young man saw the sand rising up dangerously high.

Anna looked around worriedly. She put out a foot and to her great surprise the contact with the ground was horribly painful. Her leg was stuffed with some spongy material and she would never have imagined the pain that one simple footstep could cause.

Her mind was starting to crack and she screamed louder as Richard tried to drag her with him.

"Can you get it or not?" Beffort asked, infuriated as well now. "It can't take one hour to cut the electricity."

He had just finished speaking when some Marines came running down the corridor, armed with a blowtorch.

"The juice is cut in the whole sector," the guy carrying the blowtorch said, "but apparently the door is blocked on the inside. Move away! This'll open it up in five minutes." And he bent over in front of the lock.

Behind the door the screams were fading, giving way to even more harrowing sounds. First there was the sound of crawling, a frightening, disgusting slithering sound as if a mass of flesh were slowly crossing the cabin. Then came a scream that was no longer human.

All the men, in silent terror, turned pale, looked at one another and the Marine turned off the blowtorch that he held in his trembling hands. Beffort and Yosho said nothing, also frozen in fright by the unnamable sound that came straight out of hell.

But Beffort got hold of himself. "Keep going," he ordered. "We have to see, to make sure…"

The soldier turned on the blowtorch and got back to work on the lock. After a few minutes the biggest pieces of metal fell to the ground with a loud thud. The door opened a few inches, letting loose the strong odor of rotting flesh. Beffort pushed it open all the way and the men entered the room. It was plunged in shadows and they could not see anything at first.

Beffort, who was at the head of the group, spread his arms to hold back the men behind him, as if to protect them from any possible danger. All of them froze for an instant. They were expecting an apocalyptic vision. After hearing about Richard's disappearance from the box, after smelling the foul odor of putrefaction that filled the corridors and after hearing the atrocious screams coming from the cabin, they were prepared for the worst.

When their eyes adjusted to the darkness, they saw that there was nothing to see. No body, no monster was crouching in the shadows. The cabin was calm and quiet and everything was in order.

But Anna Bernyanyi had disappeared.

"Turn on the light," Beffort said. "Is there a trap door or some other way to get out of this cabin?"

The crew answered in the negative. The room was bright now and they could see every nook and cranny in the neon light. All of a sudden Beffort rushed forward. A split second earlier he thought he had seen something on the floor. But maybe it was an illusion. He knelt down and swept his hands over the floor, searching for some unlikely clue.

"It's not possible," he stood up slowly. "We all heard the struggle. There was something inside this room. We have to search the entire sub. We've got no time to lose."

When the crew had left Yosho stepped up to his colleague. Beffort was still inspecting the cabin where Anna should be found. But it was completely empty of any human or inhuman presence.

"Richard Tardif did come into this room," Yosho said. "He came to get Anna and he took her with him."

"Yes but where?" Beffort grumbled, becoming annoyed.

"Have you noticed that the rotting stench is completely gone now?" Yosho ignored his colleague's bad mood.

Since the FBI agent did not answer Yosho continued in a calm voice. "You know very well that we won't find them on the submarine. They've gone elsewhere."

"What do you mean, Yosho?"

"You were saying before that you'd seen something weird in Nevada. That the game is being played now on a different level. What happened here seems to prove you right. Look, Smith, just now, when you squatted down, you knocked this over."

Yosho bent over and picked up an object that Beffort had knocked over in his haste. It was a frame holding a photo that Anna had kept with her, even though her blindness kept her from looking at it.

The two men stared at the picture in silence. It showed the young lady standing next to Richard Tardif. They were both smiling at the camera. The photo was not very good quality but this was not important. They saw clearly that the two of them were happy.

Chapter XV

The day before, Claude Vauzières had left Aix-en-Provence to go to his house around Nyons. He liked the small town in the Drôme and not just because it was the birthplace of his favorite writer, René Barjavel.

Claude was a big fan of Barjavel's novels and of science fiction in general. He himself wrote some and even more than just writing some said that he believed the stories he wrote. In truth, Claude Vauzières was convinced of the existence of flying saucers. He was convinced that the earth was under the control of extraterrestrials and through perseverance he had managed to win over some of his readers. He took the subject very seriously and had made several trips to the USA with some followers just to see the famous Area 51 and penetrate the mystery surrounding it.

From his overseas voyages Claude Vauzières had never brought back any proof of the existence of extraterrestrials. But he came back every time very satisfied with the nice trip, his head full of ideas, a bunch of stuff that he would use for new stories.

His last expedition dated back more than a year. He went to New Mexico, to Albuquerque with George Clinton Andrews, the famous American ufologist. Their trip had lasted more than a month. Then Claude went back to Aix-en-Provence but this time things were different. On his return he had given no conference and had announced no ufology news. Some of his friends even believed that their friend was falling into a deep depression.

Claude Vauzières spoke no more about flying saucers and his stories were now about other things. It was obviously a lot more serious than just a bad spell.

The only one to really know what had happened was his friend Olivier Raynaud, the only person whom Claude still invited occasionally to his little house in Nyons where he spent most of his free time.

One day in May, with spring colors already blooming, the two men were having a drink on the terrace of the Café des Autobus in the middle of town. Olivier once again pressed his friend, "You're going to have to talk about your discovery. Otherwise this thing is going to wear you down to nothing."

"But it's the property of the US. I found it there. The fact that I brought it back to France will bring on all kinds of trouble."

"It's incredible! In all this time that you've been interested in paranormal phenomena, for once you have real proof... Bring it back to the US, maybe it's not too late."

"I'll never go back there," Vauzières almost yelled. "I'll never set foot over there as long as that Japanese woman has still got it in her sights. I'd rather go to Corsica."

"In that case, talk to your friend George Clinton Andrews. He could get in touch with the FBI and they'll come over."

"I have absolutely no desire to see the FBI landing in the Drôme!"

"Think about it, Claude. This business is turning you in a wreck and I don't think you have much of a choice."

More than two months after the events occurred in Okinawa, the islands seemed to be calm again. Of course, the American military personnel had been greatly reduced. Two bases had been totally destroyed, others closed and specialists were working relentlessly on the ones that had been the theater of the gruesome episodes, trying to uncover the secret of the plague that had struck.

The Japanese population of Okinawa was, on the whole, satisfied to see the American army, which it had long considered an occupying force, gradually desert the territory.

On the island of Hawaii the Atomos Organization seemed to be ruined but the terrible Japanese woman had still not shown her face. Neither to claim victory nor to hurl threats at the American authorities who were lost in conjectures.

Since he, too, was lost in bewilderment, Smith Beffort was taking a break with his family. Trying to hide the marks on his face, like after every ordeal he had gone through, he was spending quality time with his child and Mie.

Beffort was busy reading books that he had never thought of opening before. Works about occultism and black magic. But everything they said was too obscure or too superficial for the agent who wanted to keep his feet on the ground despite what he had seen.

It was when he got back to the FBI building in D.C. one morning that his boss Jonathan Forbes informed him that someone living in France had been insisting on talking to him for several days. If Forbes was telling him in person, it must have been pretty important.

However, after checking the identity of the man in question, Beffort was annoyed to see he had a reputation that badly tarnished his credibility. The individual was one of those you could call a "ufo enthusiast", those who see Martians everywhere, who claim to have been in contact with extraterrestrials, who were abducted or even raped, for the luckiest of them.

"And you want me to go to France?" Beffort was astonished by his boss. "All this because some nut has something to show me? Something important concerning Madame Atomos?"

"Indeed," Forbes responded. "And especially because the guy in question won't come here under any circumstances."

Beffort was about to snap back at him when he suddenly understood what Forbes was trying to make him understand.

"Seeing that light in your eyes, I figure you agree with me, Beffort," the FBI Director said.

"Completely, Sir. Would it be possible to take my wife with me on this mission?"

"I was just going to suggest that, Beffort. We even anticipated your request. Tickets for France are ready for both of you. You'll land in Marseille and go to the town of Nyons where Claude Vauzières will be waiting for you. We booked a room in a hotel in Pontias for one month. I think that should be enough time to get all the facts. If not, you're authorized to extend your stay. You'll see the region's great for tourism so I hope Mie will appreciate it."

"Thank you, Sir. I think Mie needs a vacation as much as I do. Plus we have friends who'll be glad to watch our kid while we're gone."

"So it's done. Have a good vacation, Beffort. And above all, don't forget to bring me back a bottle of Chouchen.

Beffort and Mie soon realized that the knowledge of Jonathan Forbes concerning French specialties was far from accurate. As FBI Director, having just replaced J. Edgar Hoover (recently deceased), Forbes made it a point of honor to know everything about everything, but his experience in matters of local products in foreign countries left a lot to be desired.

The specialty of Nyons was, in fact, olive oil. As for the Chouchen requested by the director, the receptionist at the hotel and the people in town had never heard of it.

Beffort met Claude Vauzières on Friday evening at the Café des Autobus. The Frenchman was busy drinking a Ricard, the regional drink that he suggested to Beffort right away.

"I really appreciate the FBI sending one of its agents here to hear me out. And I'm glad, Monsieur Beffort, that it is you because I know your reputation."

"It seems you have some information to give me."

"Yes. Something absolutely unbelievable and it'll get you to understand the tragic events that happened on your bases in Okinawa."

"I'm used to hearing about unbelievable things, Mr. Vauvières. But I'd prefer if you didn't prolong the suspense and you get right to the point."

"Willingly. But for that you'll have to come up to my place. I live on a side street near the Tour Randonne. It's five minutes on foot. We can go right now if you'd like."

After finishing their drinks the two men walked through the steep alleys that wound around the old town of Nyons and they were soon at the square off which Claude Vauzières lived.

"You see, Monsieur Beffort, I've already been to the United States five times. In New Mexico to be precise. Although I've never seen them personally, I believe in the existence of extraterrestrials. But one day, around Albuquerque, I saw, just a few feet away from me, a small, round device. No bigger than a soccer ball and it looked nothing at all like what we generally think of as flying saucers. At first I even believed that it was a remote-controlled toy that kids play with. And then the thing came and hovered in front of me. As if intentionally. As if it was trying to tell me something. I grabbed it and that's when I noticed that there was a door in its side. And it opened. And then I saw... I saw...!"

"What did you see?"

"Come with me, I'll show you."

Vauzières led Beffort to the back of his small yard behind the house. He pointed to a flowerbed where a crude, wooden cross was sticking out. With meticulous care, like an archeologist, Claude Vauzières started digging in the soil around the little cross. And after a minute Beffort was seeing the unthinkable. And the certainty that his vacation in Provence was over and done with. He would have to return to Washington as soon as possible.

Two days later in a science lab of the FBI, Smith Beffort, who was back to work, was questioning relentlessly the researchers studying the strange object that he had brought back from France 24 hours ago.

"We're still working on it and trying to get as much information as we can from these sheets of paper," said one of the men sitting in front of the main computer. "Despite the papers' deterioration, which even an extremely precise monovision can't entirely read properly, we're still going to get a satisfactory result thanks to the gradual thermal transfer."

The man pointed to the blank pages spitting out of the machine.

"A polyester film covered with a layer of wax four to five micrometers thick, that's what's going to save your precious documents, Mr. Smith. And let us read them too. I think it'll be finished in about ten hours."

"Tell me," Jonathan Forbes said to Beffort who was sitting across from him, looking very solemn.

"This Frenchman brought me to his house after telling me his story. A story about a flying saucer floating around him. It could have been anything. A bunch of nonsense like you hear about all the time. But in this guy's garden was a tiny grave. It looked like for a cat or a rabbit. He started digging it up. And what he unearthed was a human skeleton, abnormally small, about eight inches long. A little like what was found in Okinawa. The body was dressed in an American Army uniform. The skeleton belonged to Captain Alec Craig from the main base in Okinawa. We identified it because it still had its dog tags. The Frenchman explained to me that the saucer, or rather the sphere, opened up in front of him while he was taking a walk around Albuquerque. He grabbed the body and instead of taking it to the authorities he brought it back to France. Captain Craig was already dead when he found him, which made Mr. Vauzières not want to get asked too many questions. Since he was an extraterrestrial fanatic, he figured it was too good an opportunity to pass up. And then he regretted what he did."

"Has Captain Craig been formally identified?"

"Beyond any possible doubt. He had documents on him. But documents shrunk so small we couldn't read them. They're being deciphered as we speak and the science lab is going to restore the ruined text. We'll have the results soon enough."

"Captain Craig was found inside a ship the size of a soccer ball… and it turned into a spaceship?"

"According to the Frenchman it shot directly into space at lightning speed."

A few minutes Beffort and Forbes were informed that the document had been enlarged and was readable.

It was a text that Captain Alec Craig had written by hand during his captivity and that told of the extraordinary experience he lived through in the Atomos Organization.

"I, Alec Craig, will try to catch up on the notes I took. They're short but written with all the clarity that remains to me. It's been 48 hours since I was taken prisoner by the Atomos Organization. I don't know how it happened but I do know that we went through an awful experience.

"Two days ago I was Captain on the Okinawa Air Base. I only have vague memories of what happened. A hazy memory of being half-conscious in a kind of vehicle that moved a lot and seemed to be going fast. At first I thought I was dreaming. I had a weird vision of a giant spider and other things that were unusually big but I couldn't tell what they were. Now I know.

"There are 13 of us. All Marines. I'm the only officer. As incredible as it sounds we've all been miniaturized, then brought to an unknown destination inside a kind of big crate."

"Days have gone by. I have time to write because not much happens. I'm going to die for sure. But today I want to put pen to paper because I know what really happened to us.

"I saw Madame Atomos. I spoke very little with her. But she talked more with my comrades and she seemed not to care whether I overheard or not. I am, therefore, now able to explain what happened, in the hope that someone will find this journal someday.

"From what she said, Madame Atomos has been experimenting with miniaturization for several years because she wants to shrink her flying saucers to make them weapons of war. Apparently she has succeeded.

"However, there's still one problem that, from what she said, she can't resolve: to shrink humans into an army of pilots whose size would fit into her miniature saucers. She decided to use the Marines on the Okinawa bases as guinea pigs in her experiments. For this she got a machine on the bases, a kind of cylinder tuned to different frequencies according to the bases concerned. She planned to test all the stages of the miniaturizing process.

"I guess her technique was not perfected. From what I understood there were some disastrous results. I even heard some other Organization members joking about the failures. Our base seems to be the only one where the experiment worked, despite some minor glitches. But I won't go into details. There are still 13 of us here. Somewhere completely unknown."

"For three days my comrades and I were back to normal size. Then we underwent other tests and were shrunk again and again. Seven times for me but to different sizes every time.

"Except for that we haven't been treated badly and we're well fed. There are 20 people taking care of us. I think two of them are specialized researchers. And we've seen Madame Atomos a few more times.

"The day before yesterday they brought in a sphere the size of a bowling ball. It's a remote-controlled ship that has no weapons and no identification. It's just an experimental ship meant to hold a miniaturized man. I know that this ball is a prototype of the engines of destruction that Madame Atomos wants to perfect.

"The Organization put me inside for test flights lasting up to an hour. I'm sure I traveled up into space but I couldn't see anything because there are no windows in the ship.

"Physically I'm fine. I'm in no pain. I know, however, that I should be preparing to die.

"I don't want my jailors to find these notes. I'm going to stop writing for now and hide them on me.

"I'm not being watched at the moment and I can get back to my observations. Yesterday they brought me back quickly to the experimental center. There must have been a problem with the sphere. I think they had trouble piloting it or maybe risked losing control if they sent it too far.

"For a few days I've been separated from my companions. I don't even know if they're still alive.

"As for Madame Atomos, I've seen her a few times but she didn't talk to me directly. Before being kidnapped I'd never seen this woman. But I have to say that she's not like I imagined her. I heard she'd changed how she looked, that she got younger by dematerializing. At first I thought she was really young until I noticed that she wears a mask. A totally smooth, almost rigid mask.

Only her eyes look alive. But they're eyes that give life to the whole mask.

"I don't understand everything because at times like this I don't worry about understanding. I worry about staying alive.

"I'll say that right now as I write these lines, I haven't really seen this Japanese woman's face and maybe it's better like this. Things have happened around her that I'd rather not know. I don't think it much matters whether she's dead or alive. I've seen her with my own eyes.

"There's a good chance I won't survive all these tests. And I'm almost relieved when I think of the battle that we'll soon be fighting. I wish you all good luck.

"Captain Craig."

"I think there's no doubt about the authenticity of this document," Forbes said.

"I think so too. And at least now we know where we stand."

"But do we really know who we're fighting against."

"Still the same person, Sir. There's no doubt about it. Everything in the world changes. But whatever her methods, Madame Atomos will always be Madame Atomos. Even if, in the experiments she's doing to miniaturize flying saucers and pilots, she makes a few mistakes and some Marines are transformed into living corpses, others into moving statues, others even into ectoplasms, Madame Atomos was still successful at the Okinawa Air base and the threat is still present.

Claude Vauzières was not very young. But the few times he would go down to the Café des Autobus, his friends clearly saw that he was deteriorating. The writer had taken the FBI agent to his house and shown him the corpse of the captain from space. But he had not told him everything.

He was aging and he knew that his days were numbered. Claude Vauzières believed more in the existence of flying saucers than in paradise and he felt remorse eating away at him. He had not told the FBI agent that on that day when he came in contact with the sphere, it had not soared up into the sky at lightning speed. No, in fact, the sphere had simply stopped working. And Vauzières quickly snatched it up just as he did the captain's body.

The broken down sphere was in his house in Nyons. The ufologist did not really expect to see it flying again but he loved to think about having an extraterrestrial spaceship at home. For now and until the end of his life the sphere was a source of joy and the symbol of his guilty conscience. He died peacefully less than a year after his meeting with Smith Beffort. When his children came to take inventory of his belongings in the little house sitting in the medieval village, they paid no attention to the weird sphere that was over the neighbor's yard as one of their children must have thought it was a balloon and shot at it. And since Nyons is a town in the hills, the small round object drifted down, slowly but surely, into the town square.

Today the sphere still has not been picked up by the Nyons street sweepers because every time they come by it ends up stuck in a corner where nobody can see it.

A customer sitting on the terrace of a café in the Place des Arcades could easily see the children in the town using it for their never-ending soccer games.

Because in Nyons, America is far away and Madame Atomos just a legend for certain specialists.

And because Nyons is also the town where René Barjavel was born.

Updated Timeline

By Jean-Marc Lofficier

1911.
Probable birth of Kanoto Yoshimuta in Nagasaki. (She is 50 years-old in 1961 when Yosho Akamatsu conducts his first investigation.)

Until 1930.
The Way of the Crane. Friendly relations between the Yoshimuta and Hayashi families. (Kato Hayashi leaves Japan to serve the Green Hornet around 1930.)

1931.
Beginning of Japanese imperialism; invasion of Manchuria.

Date unknown. Kanoto is admitted to the University of Nagasaki; she is extremely gifted, especially in physics and biology.

1933.
The Red Silk Scarf. Kanoto meets Harry Dickson.

Date unknown. Kanoto marries (probably a colleague) and has at least two children.

1937.
Invasion of China by the Japanese.
The Butterfly Files. Kanoto and her husband help the war effort by joining (possibly heading) the Noborito

Research Institute, a secret military laboratory devoted to atomic, bacteriological and chemical research.

1938.
(*January*) Occupation of Nanking by the Japanese.
The Butterfly Files. The Japanese obtain Dr. Fu Man-chu's notes on his biological and chemical experiments, and forward them to the Noborito Research Institute.

1939.
(*December*) *Before the War, Five Dragons Roar*. On a ship crossing the Pacific, Kanoto meets Charlie Chan and Mr. Moto.

1941.
(7 December) Attack on Pearl Harbor.

1944.
(*October*) *The Butterfly Files*. Start of correspondence between Kanoto and Shiro Ishii, director of Unit 731 in Manchuria.

1945.
(*May*) *The Butterfly Files*. Kanoto writes to Ishii to inform him of the success of some of her research, but too late to change the course of the war.
(*6 August*) Destruction of Hiroshima.
(*9 August*) Destruction of Nagasaki. Kanoto escapes death, though her husband and her family perish.
(*August 15th*) Japanese surrender.
(*16-30 August*) *The Atomos Affair*. OSS agent Alexander Waverly helps Kanoto to leave Nagasaki.
(*30 August*) *The Butterfly Files*. Kanoto writes to Ishii to inform him that she has been able to preserve her re-

search and that the struggle against the United States is just beginning.

(*October*) *The Butterfly Files*. Kanoto brings together other scientists, Nazis and Japanese, including Professor Aldridge, who will provide her with the designs of her future "flying saucers".

(*November*) *Who Made Me Such A Woman?* In the ruins of Tokyo, Kanoto meets Mr. Moto and chooses her future nom-de-guerre—Madame Atomos.

1946-1950.

Kanoto teaches physics at the University of Nagasaki; Secretly, she builds her organization and continues her research.

1947.

(*September*) *Mme Atomos Bets on Death*. Bender meets Yoni in Tokyo.

1951.

Kanoto resigns from her teaching position and leaves Nagasaki.

1951-1960.

Mme Atomos prepares her future campaign against the United States. She sends teams of agents to build secret bases on American soil, occupies Atomia Island and builds its Great Brain and flying city.

1960.

With the Compliments of Nestor Burma! In Paris, the Atomos Organization crosses the path of Nestor Burma.

1961.

Mme Atomos attracts the attention of the Japanese authorities in Sasebo, where one of its bases and a test of her disintegrating ray are discovered. The Tokkoka orders Yosho Akamatsu to open an investigation.

1962.

The Mystery of *Mororan*. Second test of the disintegrating ray. Mme. Atomos is finally ready to attack the United States.

1963.

(*February*) *The Sinister Mme Atomos*. FBI agent Sam Forbes discovers the threat of Mme Atomos. He is killed and replaced by Smith Beffort and Dr. Alan Soblen.
Mie Azusa, a singing student at Takarazuka school in Tokyo, is kidnapped by Mme Atomos, transported to Atomia, and operated on to become Miss Atomos.
(*July*) *The Butterfly Files*. Beginning of William Mulder's investigation into Mme Atomos.
(*Summer*) *The Most Dreadful Monster*. Mme Atomos kidnaps Bruce Banner.
(*November*) *Mme Atomos' Xmas*. Mme Atomos organizes JFK's assassination.

1964.

(*February*) *Mme Atomos Sows Terror*. Mme Atomos attacks Texas.
(*Spring*) *The Woman in the High Castle*. Mme Atomos learns of a parallel universe in which Japan won the war.
(*September*) *Mme Atomos Srikes at the Head*. Fake death of Mme Atomos in San Francisco. Creation of the American Organization of The Friends of Mme Atomos.
(*November*) Election of President Lyndon B. Johnson.

1965.

(*February*) *Miss Atomos*. Mie strikes in Florida, then falls in love with Smith. Death of the Boss of the FBI, replaced by John Edward Evans.

(*July*) *The Butterfly Files*. William Mulder's report complete.

(*September*) *Miss Atomos vs. The KKK*. Mie, now free from Mme Atomos' control, becomes pregnant. Mme Atomos returns.

(*9 November*) *The Atomos Affair*. A power failure plunged the East Coast into darkness. Mme Atomos enters UNCLE's HQ to talk to Alexander Waverly.

1966.

(*January*) *The Return of Mme Atomos*. Creation of the Green Dragon force to fight Mme Atomos. Smith and Mie flee to France.

(*April*) *The End of the Brotherhood of the Sword*. Birth of Robert "Bob" Beffort at the American Hospital in Neuilly near Paris.

(*May-June*) *The Mistake of Mme Atomos*. The Befforts return to the US. Destruction of Mme Atomos's flying city.

(*July*) Mme Atomos prepares her attack on Rhode Island.

(*August*) *The Way of the Crane*. Mme Atomos meets with Kato Hayashi in Hiroshima.

1967.

(*January-February*) *Mme Atomos Prolongs Life*. Mme Atomos strikes in Rhode Island, spreading the "disease" of immortality.

(*July*) *The Monsters of Mme Atomos*. Mme Atomos turns the inhabitants of Baltimore into monsters.

(*August*) *Mme Atomos Spits Fire*. Mme Atomos sets fire to Nevada. Her successive dematerializations cause her to rejuvenate.

(*November-December*) *The Revenge of Mme Atomos*. Destruction of Atomia Island and the Atomos organization. Mme Atomos murders Dr. Soblen and Bob Beffort.

1968.

(*January*) Tet Offensive in Vietnam.

(*February*) *The Evil of Mme Atomos*. Mie pursues Mme Atomos in Montana.

(*May*) *The Resurrection of Mme Atomos*. Mme Atomos is now fully rejuvenated.

(*June*) *The Seduction of Mme Atomos*. Mme Atomos use her new-found charms to seduce Yosho.

(*September-October*) *The Mark of Mme Atomos*. Destruction of a new Atomos laboratory in Oakland.

(*November*) First election of President Richard M. Nixon.

(*December*) *The Cold War of Mme Atomos*. Mme Atomos uses a freezer to spread terror, travels to Mexico and meets Isadori.

1969.

(*April*) *The Slaves of Mme Atomos*. Mme Atomos develops a new mind control technique. Suicide of John Edward Evans.

(*20 July*) *On an Ill Wind...* Neil Armstrong unknowingly plants Mme Atomos' flag on the Moon.

Jonathan Forbes (Sam's younger brother) replaces Evans.

(*8 August*) Sharon Tate's murder.

1970.

(*May-July*) *Mme Atomos Sows the Whirlwind*. Mme Atomos exacerbates generational conflicts in Los Angeles. Dr. Creighton replaces Dr. Soblen.

(*November*) *Mme Atomos Bets on Death*. Mme Atomos threatens Las Vegas with a nuclear attack. Birth of Dawn Beffort, Smith and Mie's daughter.

1972.

(*spring*) *The Sins of Mme Atomos*. Mme Atomos attacks Okinawa.

(*June*) *A Day in the Life of Mme Atomos*. Mme Atomos recuperates in London.

(*17 June*) Watergate burglary.

(*November*) Reelection of President Nixon.

1973.

(*January*) Signing of the Paris Accords; end of the Vietnam War.

1974.

(*9 August*) President Nixon resigns.

1975.

(*April*) Fall of Saigon

1976.

(*January*) *Mme Atomos' Holidays*. Mme Atomos benefits from the Yellow Shadow's help and steals Howard Hughes' fortune to rebuild her organization.

(*June-October*) *Mme Atomos Fait Parler les Morts* (untranslated). Mme Atomos launches a zombie attack on

New York. First clues that she may have moved her base of operations to the Dark Side of the Moon.
(*November*) Election of President Jimmy Carter.

1978.
The Spheres of Mme Atomos. Mrs. Atomos attacks again, using small miniature spherical vessels.

SF & FANTASY

Adolphe Alhaiza. *Cybele*

Alphonse Allais. *The Adventures of Captain Cap*

Henri Allorge. *The Great Cataclysm*

Guy d'Armen. *Doc Ardan: The City of Gold and Lepers; The Troglodytes of Mount Everest/The Giants of Black Lake; The Abominable Snowman*

G.-J. Arnaud. *The Ice Company*

André Arnyvelde. *The Ark; The Mutilated Bacchus*

Charles Asselineau. *The Double Life*

Henri Austruy. *The Eupantophone; The Olotelepan; The Petitpaon Era*

Barillet-Lagargousse. *The Final War*

Barbot de Villeneuve.*The Naiads/Beauty & The Beast*

Cyprien Bérard. *The Vampire Lord Ruthwen*

S. Henry Berthoud. *Martyrs of Science; The Angel Asrael*

Aloysius Bertrand. *Gaspard de la Nuit*

Richard Bessière. *The Gardens of the Apocalypse; The Masters of Silence*

Chevalier de Béthune. *The World of Mercury*

Albert Bleunard. *Ever Smaller*

Félix Bodin. *The Novel of the Future*

Pierre Boitard. *Journey to the Sun*

Louis Boussenard. *Monsieur Synthesis*

Alphonse Brown. *City of Glass; The Conquest of the Air*

Émile Calvet. *In a Thousand Years*

André Caroff. *The Terror of Madame Atomos; Miss Atomos; The Return of Madame Atomos; The Mistake of Madame Atomos; The Monsters of Madame Atomos; The Revenge of Madame Atomos; The Resurrection of Madame Atomos; The Mark of Madame Atomos; The Spheres of Madame Atomos; The Wrath of Madame Atomos* (w/M. & Sylvie Stéphan)

Jean Carrère. *The End of Atlantis*

Félicien Champsaur. *Homo-Deus; The Human Arrow; Nora, The Ape-Woman; Ouha, King of the Apes; Pharaoh's Wife*

Didier de Chousy. *Ignis*

Jules Clarétie. *Obsession*

Jacques Collin de Plancy. *Voyage to the Center of the Earth*

Michel Corday. *The Eternal Flame; The Lynx* (w/André Couvreur)
André Couvreur. *Caresco, Superman; The Exploits of Professor Tornada* (3 vols.); *The Necessary Evil*
Gaston Danville. *The Perfume of Lust*
Camille Debans. *The Misfortunes of John Bull*
Captain Danrit. *Undersea Odyssey*
C. I. Defontenay. *Star (Psi Cassiopeia)*
Charles Derennes. *The People of the Pole*
Georges Dodds (anthologist). *The Missing Link*
Charles Dodeman. *The Silent Bomb*
Harry Dickson. *The Heir of Dracula; Harry Dickson vs. The Spider*
Jules Dornay. *Lord Ruthven Begins*
Alfred Driou. *The Adventures of a Parisian Aeronaut*
Odette Dulac. *The War of the Sexes*
Alexandre Dumas. *The Return of Lord Ruthven; The Man who Married a Mermaid* (w/P. Lacroix)
Renée Dunan. *Baal; The Ultimate Pleasure*
J.-C. Dunyach. *The Night Orchid; The Thieves of Silence*
Henri Duvernois. *The Man Who Found Himself*
Achille Eyraud. *Voyage to Venus*
Henri Falk. *The Age of Lead*
Paul Féval. *Anne of the Isles; Knightshade; Revenants; Vampire City; The Vampire Countess; The Wandering Jew's Daughter*
Paul Féval, *fils. Felifax, the Tiger-Man*
Charles de Fieux. *Lamékis*
Fernand Fleuret. *Jim Click*
Charles-Marie Flor O'Squarr. *Phantoms*
Louis Forest. *Someone is Stealing Children in Paris*
Arnould Galopin. *Doctor Omega; Doctor Omega and the Shadowmen* (anthology)
Judith Gautier. *Isoline and the Serpent-Flower*
H. Gayar. *The Marvelous Adventures of Serge Myrandhal on Mars*
Louis Geoffroy. *The Apocryphal Napoleon*
G.L. Gick. *Harry Dickson and the Werewolf of Rutherford Grange*
Raoul Gineste. *The Second Life of Doctor Albin*
Delphine de Girardin. *Balzac's Cane*
Léon Gozlan. *The Vampire of the Val-de-Grâce*
Jules Gros. *The Fossil Man*
Jimmy Guieu. *The Polarian-Denebian War* (2 vols.)
Edmond Haraucourt. *Daah, the First Human; Illusions of Immortality*
Nathalie Henneberg. *The Green Gods*

Eugène Hennebert. *The Enchanted City*

Jules Hoche. *The Maker of Men and His Formula*

V. Hugo, P. Foucher & P. Meurice. *The Hunchback of Notre-Dame*

Romain d'Huissier. *Hexagon: Dark Matter*

Jules Janin. *The Magnetized Corpse*

Gustave Kahn. *The Tale of Gold and Silence*

Gérard Klein. *The Mote in Time's Eye*

Fernand Kolney. *Love in 5000 Years*

Paul Lacroix. *Danse Macabre; The Man who Married a Mermaid* (w/Alexandre Dumas)

Louis-Guillaume de La Follie. *The Unpretentious Philosopher*

Jean de La Hire. *The Fiery Wheel; Enter the Nyctalope; The Nyctalope on Mars; The Nyctalope vs. Lucifer; The Nyctalope Steps In; Night of the Nyctalope; Return of the Nyctalope*

Etienne-Léon de Lamothe-Langon. *The Virgin Vampire*

André Laurie. *Spiridon*

Gabriel de Lautrec. *The Vengeance of the Oval Portrait*

Alain le Drimeur. *The Future City*

Georges Le Faure & Henri de Graffigny. *The Extraordinary Adventures of a Russian Scientist Across the Solar System* (2 vols.)

Gustave Le Rouge. *The Dominion of the World* (w/Gustave Guitton) (4 vols.); *The Mysterious Doctor Cornelius* (3 vols.); *The Vampires of Mars*

Jules Lermina. *The Battle of Strasbourg; Mysteryville; Panic in Paris; The Secret of Zippelius; To-Ho and the Gold Destroyers*

Maurice Level. *The Gates of Hell*

André Lichtenberger. *The Centaurs; The Children of the Crab*

Maurice Limat. *Mephista*

Listonai. *The Philosophical Voyager*

Jean-Marc & Randy Lofficier. *Edgar Allan Poe on Mars; The Katrina Protocol; Pacifica 1, 2; Robonocchio; Return of the Nyctalope;* (anthologists) *Tales of the Shadowmen 1-13; The Vampire Almanac* (2 vols.)

Ch. Lomon & P.-B. Gheuzi. *The Last Days of Atlantis*

Charles Malato. *Lost!*

Maurice Magre. *The Marvelous Story of Claire d'Amour; The Call of the Beast; Priscilla of Alexandria; The Angel of Lust*

Camille Mauclair. *The Virgin Orient*

Xavier Mauméjean. *The League of Heroes*

Joseph Méry. *The Tower of Destiny*

Hippolyte Mettais. *Paris Before the Deluge; The Year 5865*

Louise Michel. *The Human Microbes; The New World*
Tony Moilin. *Paris in the Year 2000*
Michael Moorcock's *Legends of the Multiverse*
José Moselli. *Illa's End*
John-Antoine Nau. *Enemy Force*
Marie Nizet. *Captain Vampire*
Charles Nodier. *Trilby and The Crumb Fairy*
C. Nodier, A. Beraud & Toussaint-Merle. *Frankenstein*
Henri de Parville. *An Inhabitant of the Planet Mars*
Gaston de Pawlowski. *Journey to the Land of the 4th Dimension*
Georges Pellerin. *The World in 2000 Years*
Ernest Pérochon. *The Frenetic People*
Pierre Pelot. *The Child Who Walked on the Sky*
Jean Petithuguenin. *An International Mission to the Moon*
J. Polidori, C. Nodier, E. Scribe. *Lord Ruthven the Vampire*
P.-A. Ponson du Terrail. *The Immortal Woman; The Vampire and the Devil's Son; The Police Agent*
Georges Price. *The Missing Men of the* Sirius
René Pujol. *The Chimerical Quest*
Edgar Quinet. *Ahasuerus; The Enchanter Merlin*
Jean Rameau. *Arrival; in the Stars*
Henri de Régnier. *A Surfeit of Mirrors*
Maurice Renard. *The Blue Peril; Doctor Lerne; The Doctored Man; A Man Among the Microbes; The Master of Light*
Restif de la Bretonne. *The Discovery of the Austral Continent by a Flying Man; Posthumous Correspondence* (3 vols.); *The Fay Ouroucoucou* (2 vols.)
Jean Richepin. *The Crazy Corner; The Wing*
Albert Robida. *The Adventures of Saturnin Farandoul; Chalet in the Sky; The Clock of the Centuries; The Electric Life; The Engineer Von Satanas*
J.-H. Rosny Aîné. *Helgvor of the Blue River; The Givreuse Enigma; The Mysterious Force; The Navigators of Space; Vamireh; The World of the Variants; The Young Vampire*
Marcel Rouff. *Journey to the Inverted World*
Marie-Anne de Roumier-Robert. *The Voyage of Lord Seaton to the Seven Planets*
Léonie Rouzade. *The World Turned Upside Down*
Han Ryner. *The Human Ant; The Superhumans*
Henri de Saint-Georges. *The Green Eyes*
Louis-Claude de Saint-Martin. *The Crocodile*

Frank Schildiner. *The Quest of Frankenstein; The Triumph of Frankenstein; Napoleon's Vampire Hunters*

Nicolas Ségur. *The Human Paradise*

Pierre de Selenes: *An Unknown World*

Norbert Sevestre. *Sâr Dubnotal: Vs. Jack the Ripper; The Astral Trail*

Angelo de Sorr. *The Vampires of London*

Brian Stableford. *The Empire of the Necromancers (1. The Shadow of Frankenstein; 2. Frankenstein and the Vampire Countess; 3. Frankenstein in London); The Wayward Muse; Eurydice's Lament; The Mirror of Dionysius; The New Faust at the Tragicomique; Sherlock Holmes and The Vampires of Eternity; The Stones of Camelot* (anthologist) *News from the Moon; The Germans on Venus; The Supreme Progress; The World Above the World; Nemoville; Investigations of the Future; The Conqueror of Death; The Revolt of the Machines; The Man With the Blue Face; The Aerial Valley; The New Moon; The Nickel Man; On the Brink of the World's End; The Mirror of Present Events; The Humanisphere*

Jacques Spitz. *The Eye of Purgatory*

Kurt Steiner. *Ortog*

Eugène Thébault. *Radio-Terror*

C.-F. Tiphaigne de La Roche. *Amilec*

Simon Tyssot de Patot. *The Strange Voyages of Jacques Massé and Pierre de Mésange*

Louis Ulbach. *Prince Bonifacio*

Théo Varlet. *The Castaways of Eros; The Golden Rock.; The Martian Epic* (w/Octave Joncquel); *Timeslip Troopers* (w/André Blandin); *The Xenobiotic Invasion*

Pierre Véron. *The Merchants of Health*

Paul Vibert. *The Mysterious Fluid*

Villiers de l'Isle-Adam. *The Scaffold; The Vampire Soul*

Gaston de Wailly. *The Murderer of the World*

Philippe Ward. *Artahe; Manhattan Ghost* (w/Mickael Laguerre); *The Song of Montségur* (w/Sylvie Miller)

Victor Margueritte. *The Bacheloress; The Companion; The Couple*